FROM THE
NANCY DREW FILES

THE CASE: Searching for a stolen painting, Nancy draws a portrait of an elusive master thief.

CONTACT: Michael Jared's painting The Kiss is missing. Can Nancy fill the void?

SUSPECTS: Debbie Lakin—The assistant curator of the museum, she turned off the alarm system the night of the theft . . . and refuses to say why.

Bryan Barbour—Ned's fraternity brother, he's an expert at rope climbing . . . a skill used by the thief to get in and out of the museum unnoticed.

Rina O'Neill—Bryan left her to date Debbie, and Rina may have stolen the painting in order to frame her rival.

COMPLICATIONS: Michael Jared lost his prized painting, and in helping him to recover The Kiss, Nancy could risk losing Ned!

Books in The Nancy Drew Files® Series

The NANCY DREW

Files™

111

THE
STOLEN KISS

CAROLYN KEENE

AN ARCHWAY PAPERBACK
Published by POCKET BOOKS
New York   London   Toronto   Sydney   Tokyo   Singapore

This book is a work of fiction. Names, characters, places and incidents are products of the author's imagination or are used fictitiously. Any resemblance to actual events or locales or persons, living or dead, is entirely coincidental.

AN ARCHWAY PAPERBACK *Original*

An Archway Paperback published by
POCKET BOOKS, a division of Simon & Schuster Inc.
1230 Avenue of the Americas, New York, NY 10020

Copyright © 1995 by Simon & Schuster Inc.
Produced by Mega-Books, Inc.

ISBN: 0-671-88202-3

First Archway Paperback printing October 1995

10 9 8 7 6 5 4 3 2 1

Cover art by Cliff Miller

Printed in the U.S.A.

IL 6+

THE
STOLEN KISS

Chapter

One

WHERE IN THE WORLD is Ned Nickerson?" Eighteen-year-old Nancy Drew asked her friend George Fayne as the two girls crossed the Emerson College commons.

"Haven't a clue," George teased. "But that shouldn't stop you, Nan."

Nancy laughed, then readjusted her small green backpack, wishing for even the slightest breeze. Even in sandals, denim cutoffs, and a light sea green T-shirt, she was sweltering.

Although it was almost nine P.M., most of the students had been driven out of their dorms and onto the moonlit lawn by the September heat wave. Radios, beach blankets, and pizza boxes added to the party atmosphere, which suited Nancy perfectly.

This was a great weekend to be visiting. Her boyfriend Ned's fraternity, Omega Chi Epsilon, was hosting a Roaring Twenties party Friday night, and Sunday was the gala opening of artist Michael Jared's work at the school's museum.

George pulled her baseball cap down low over her short dark curls and scanned the commons. She snapped her fingers. "I bet Ned's in the library. It's air-conditioned."

"All right, George," Nancy cheered.

The two girls turned onto the path for the library, and George motioned Nancy to stop before they went in. She spoke to Nancy very seriously. "I probably shouldn't butt in, but I know you haven't seen Ned or had much time for him lately. I just think you shouldn't take a great guy like him for granted."

Nancy's high spirits sank a little. "I know I do take him for granted sometimes. I try not to, but it happens. I do love him but forget to show it." Nancy bit her lip. "Maybe I can make up for some of that this weekend."

George hugged Nancy. "I'm sure Ned's so happy you're here for a fun no-work weekend, he'll forget how long it's been since you've spent time together."

Nancy pushed through the library doors and stepped into the air-conditioned silence. Almost immediately she spotted Ned studying by the window, and her heart skipped a beat. "There he is."

George started toward him but Nancy pulled her back. "Let's surprise him!"

George returned Nancy's grin. "Since he's not expecting us until tomorrow, I'd say he's in for a big one." George pulled her cap down even lower and hid behind some shelves.

Stifling a giggle, Nancy tiptoed through the maze of tables and shelves, her heart beating double-time. How close could she get before Ned spotted her?

His head was bent slightly as he focused on the book open in front of him. Nancy tiptoed closer. She caught her reflection in the darkened window and fluffed out her hair. Just then Ned glanced up at the window. His eyes widened with surprise, and a huge smile spread over his handsome face.

He shot out of his chair. "Nancy!" He scooped her up in his arms and spun her around. "What are you doing here? It's only Thursday." He put her down but kept his hands on her waist.

The librarian cleared her throat, and Nancy tried to subdue her laughter. "Nice to see you, too!" She smiled up into his deep brown eyes.

Nancy took his hand and squeezed it tight. "I finished my investigation for Dad a little early," she said, referring to her father, lawyer Carson Drew. "And George was free." Nancy gestured at George peeking out from behind a bookcase. Ned's eyes flashed George a warm hello. "Bess is off with her parents on a trip," Nancy explained.

3

Bess Marvin was Nancy's other best friend and George's cousin.

"Too bad," said Ned. "Bess loves a party."

"So I called the Theta Pi house," she continued as Ned began to gather his books. "I spoke to Mindy Kwong. She said we could come a day early. We dropped our bags at the sorority and came looking for you." Nancy paused. "Do you mind?"

Ned stopped packing his books. "Are you kidding," he said softly, and turned to kiss her gently. In Ned Nickerson's arms, Nancy felt like the luckiest girl in the world.

Ned slung his backpack over one shoulder and guided Nancy toward George and the door. While Ned and George exchanged a friendly hug, Nancy flipped through a display rack filled with flyers for campus activities. "Here's a pamphlet for the museum," she said, tucking one into her pocket.

Outside, Ned turned away from the brightly lit quad and moved down a small moonlit footpath. "Let's take a shortcut back to Greek Row. Then we can go for ice cream."

"Now you're talking," George said.

As the trio was sauntering along the narrow pathway, Nancy suddenly felt someone whiz up close beside her.

"Hey!" Nancy barely kept her balance as the skater's oversize backpack grazed her arm. She glared at the hooded figure retreating in the dark.

"You okay, Nan?" Ned asked.

"Fine," Nancy assured him. She watched the in-line skater vanish around a curve in the path.

"That person was crazy," George commented. "The path's hard to see at night. How can he skate on it?"

Nancy shrugged and wondered why anyone would be in such a rush at that hour and in that heat.

They were soon passing below the art museum. The darkened glass-and-concrete building was perched on the hill above them bathed in moonlight. "I can't wait for the art gala Sunday," Nancy said.

"I can't believe we'll really get to see Michael Jared in person," George said.

Ned groaned. *"All* the girls are saying that." He ran his fingers through his dark hair. "You'd think he was a rock star, not an artist-in-residence."

Nancy flashed Ned a wicked grin. "You can't blame them. He looks like a rock star. His picture was on the cover of *Art Today.*"

"Not to mention the cover of that pamphlet you snatched up back at the library," George reminded her.

"Oh," Nancy said innocently. "I hadn't noticed."

"Since when does River Heights's star detective not notice something," Ned remarked.

Before Nancy could shoot back a reply, the museum on the hill grabbed her full attention. It had become flooded with light.

"Hey, what's going on?" George asked.

"I don't know," Ned answered. "My frat brother Bryan is a guard at the museum. He was expecting a quiet night."

A siren wailed in the distance. Minutes later a police car zoomed up the steep museum road, its red and blue lights whirling. "Trouble," Nancy announced. Without a second's hesitation she took off, sprinting up the steep stone steps to the museum with Ned and George close behind her. The police car was now at the entrance to the museum, its doors flung wide. Parked right next to the police car was a shiny black sports car. Light flooded out from the museum's massive doors.

Nancy raced into the grand foyer, with Ned and George close behind. Though all the lights were on, the hall was empty. Loud voices came from the gallery just ahead. Nancy hurried to investigate, but stopped at the gallery entrance.

Two uniformed police officers prowled the far side of the brightly lit gallery, their backs to the entrance. Two other men and a petite blond woman about Nancy's age were staring at a blank spot on the far wall. Nancy could see two hooks where a painting had once hung.

"There's been a robbery," Nancy gasped.

"This is the Jared gallery!" Ned exclaimed.

"One of his paintings was stolen before the opening?" George sounded horrified.

"It looks that way," Nancy said.

Nancy glanced around the room. A bright pink

and blue rope was dangling from a shattered ceiling skylight. Glass shards littered the floor. "That's how they got in," she said.

Nancy knew the burly man in the tweed jacket was Dean Jarvis, but the overweight man next to him was unfamiliar. She asked Ned who he was.

"Dr. Morrison, the museum curator."

"And who's the girl?"

"Debbie Lakin," Ned replied softly. "She's a Theta Pi, a transfer from Montana State last spring. She's an art history major and the museum's assistant curator, which has always been a student position."

That explained the girl's professional-looking outfit, Nancy realized. Debbie was extremely well groomed for a student, in a sleek cream-colored suit and high heels. Even with her blond hair swept up in a sophisticated twist, she most resembled a scared little girl, though.

Just then Dean Jarvis turned to the entrance and recognized Nancy. "Nancy Drew, am I glad you're here," he said, and gestured the three into the gallery. When the police officers turned around, Nancy instantly recognized the tall wiry one as Sergeant Weinberg. They had worked on earlier cases together.

Debbie Lakin smiled weakly at Ned as Sergeant Weinberg greeted Nancy warmly.

"What was stolen?" Nancy asked him. At her words the curator turned to face her. Dr. Morrison was bearded, but underneath, his face was ashen.

7

"The centerpiece of the Jared exhibit," he replied tersely. *"First Kiss.* The most valuable piece in our Jared collection." He seemed about to go on, then stopped himself and squinted suspiciously at Nancy. "Who are you?"

Dean Jarvis introduced Nancy and Ned, and Ned introduced George.

Dr. Morrison stared at the rope dangling from the ceiling. Suddenly he slapped it. "I requested a new security system months ago, Jarvis," he said, angrily. "Now look what's happened."

Dean Jarvis shifted awkwardly from one foot to the other and sighed. "We've never been burgled before. Our present security system seemed adequate."

"Why did the current system fail?" Nancy asked.

"Because it secures only the museum doors and ground-floor windows. Not the skylight, that's why," Dr. Morrison snapped. Then he shifted his gaze to Debbie. His pale gray eyes narrowed accusingly.

"Wait a minute. . . . The security system wasn't even on." He stepped closer to Debbie. "Why?"

Debbie cowered slightly and stared at the floor. "I turned it off for a moment," she mumbled.

Nancy leaned closer to listen. Why was Debbie so scared?

"Just for a second," Debbie continued, her voice quavering, "so I could leave the building.

Then I went back to the storage room to check on something and I forgot—"

"You forgot?" Dr. Morrison bellowed. "You forgot? And why are you here so late anyway? You should have left the museum hours ago."

"Umm, I—I was in the storage room working on inventory," Debbie began shakily. "Those paintings that we're selling to that dealer in New York to raise funds—"

Dr. Morrison cut her off. "What about that shipment?"

"I wanted to update the inventory before the shipment goes out next week, and I lost track of time."

"You were working on inventory this late at night?" Dr. Morrison scoffed.

Nancy eyed Debbie closely. She sensed Debbie was hiding something.

"Nancy," Dean Jarvis broke in, "you've solved cases for Emerson before. Would you consider looking into this robbery as our representative?"

Nancy took a deep breath and gazed at Ned. He met her glance and slowly shook his head. Nancy looked at him helplessly. She knew how disappointed he'd be if she spent the weekend sleuthing instead of partying with him. Nancy knew because she'd be disappointed, too.

Her resolve to stay out of it wavered. She paused and blew out a breath. She could never resist solving a mystery. "Okay," she told the dean. "You can count on me."

Ned managed a halfhearted smile.

George groaned softly.

"Thank you, Nancy," said the dean. He turned to Dr. Morrison. "Nancy Drew has been of tremendous service to Emerson in the past," he explained. Dr. Morrison nodded solemnly. Sergeant Weinberg smiled at Nancy. "Welcome on board, again," the officer said. "We'll give you all the cooperation you need."

"Great." Nancy turned to Debbie. "How did you discover the theft?" she asked.

"Oh—I didn't!" Debbie protested.

Dean Jarvis cut in. "Dr. Morrison and I did. After dinner Geoff—Dr. Morrison, that is— offered to give me a preview of the show. We discovered the burglary and called the police."

"I see," Nancy said thoughtfully. "But, Debbie, didn't you hear anything? You were in the museum."

"No. Nothing," Debbie insisted. "I told Sergeant Weinberg that."

Skirting the shards of glass, Nancy walked back under the skylight. She ran her fingers up and down the rope. "George, you've done rock climbing. Isn't this a climber's rope?"

George nodded, then fingered the rope gently. "A new one. You can see the tracks the jumars made—the gadgets you use when you climb up the rope. Otherwise the rope's barely been used."

Nancy studied the little marks closely and turned to George again. "Would it take an experienced climber to manage this height?"

"To make the climb *fast?* You bet."

"My frat brother Bryan is an experienced climber," Ned offered. "He may be able to give you some leads, Nancy." Suddenly Ned became worried. Nancy knew exactly what he was thinking.

"Where is Bryan?" she asked quietly.

Dr. Morrison gasped. "Bryan? The security guard. He's gone!"

"We'd better find him," Nancy said urgently. "He could be hurt."

Sergeant Weinberg and his partner set off to search the interior of the museum. Nancy, George, and Ned headed outside. Nancy and Ned went in opposite directions on the stone path that snaked through the museum gardens, while George circled the building.

The moon was full and high in the sky, so Nancy could see quite clearly. As she scoured the well-tended flower beds, she found no sign of the missing guard. She met Ned by the rosebushes at the far end of the garden. "Not a thing, Nan," Ned declared.

Just then a scream pierced the night.

Ned grabbed Nancy's arm. "It's George!" Nancy cried.

"Nancy! Ned! Help me!"

Chapter

Two

Nancy and Ned raced toward the sound of the screaming. "She's behind the museum!" Ned shouted over his shoulder.

A tall young man had George pinned against the building, trying to wrestle her to the ground.

"Let her go!" Nancy yelled.

"Bryan!" Ned shouted. "Leave her alone. She's a friend, George Fayne."

The young man peered at Ned but didn't let George go right away. "Ned?" He squinted into the shadows. "What are you doing here?"

"Looking for *you*, Barbour!"

Bryan finally loosened his grip on George and stepped out of the shadows. He was breathing hard from the struggle, but he was muscular and very fit. Under other circumstances Nancy would have found him very handsome.

12

George bent forward and placed her hands on her knees trying to catch her breath. Nancy stared daggers at Bryan Barbour. He caught Nancy's eye and quickly shifted his gaze back to Ned.

When George straightened up, she glared at Bryan. "Don't bother to apologize."

Bryan smoothed back his ponytail and fingered the small gold earring he wore in his left ear. His hand was shaking, and Nancy noticed that one of his fingers was freshly cut. "Sorry I freaked out that way—I really could have hurt you." He sounded confused and upset. "But what were you doing creeping around outside the museum storeroom?"

"I saw an open window into the room and thought it might have something to do with the way the thief got out. So I tried scaling the wall as the thief had done to get in."

Nancy looked above George's head. Decorative bricks poked out from the concrete. Convenient hand- and footholds for George—or the burglar.

"Thief?" Bryan gaped at George. "What thief?"

"Someone broke into the museum," Ned told him.

Bryan suddenly slumped back against the wall. "So *that's* what happened."

Before he could say more, a flashlight beam bobbed around the corner. At that very moment someone inside the museum flicked on the back floodlights, the sudden glare blinding them all.

"What's happening back here?" Sergeant Weinberg's voice preceded him around the corner.

"Everything's fine!" Nancy yelled quickly as the wiry officer came into view, his hand on the gun holstered at his side.

Behind the sergeant the other officer led the group from inside the museum: Debbie, Dean Jarvis, and a scowling Dr. Morrison.

"Barbour!" Dr. Morrison shouted. "Where have you been? We were robbed and *you* weren't around to call in the alarm."

"It wasn't my fault," Bryan said.

Sergeant Weinberg spoke quietly. "Then perhaps you can explain where you've been since you last checked in with the security company."

"Locked in a shed." Bryan motioned toward the back of the garden. "I was on my rounds when I noticed the shed door was open. I went in to check it out. Next thing I knew someone had pulled the door closed behind me and locked it."

"It has a padlock, which needs a key," added Dr. Morrison ruefully. "The thief probably knew that."

"Right." Bryan looked relieved that the curator backed up his story.

"How'd you get out?" Ned inquired. Nancy, her arm around Ned's shoulder, listened to Bryan's answer.

"With this—" Bryan produced a small Swiss

14

army knife from his pocket. "I pried off the door hinges, which luckily were on the inside. I didn't bother to yell. I figured no one would hear me—except whoever had locked me in." He gave a nervous laugh.

"Which shed?" Nancy asked.

Bryan led them to a shabby wooden structure beyond and half-hidden by the garden. The door was fastened on one side with a metal latch but had been pried off on the other side. Bryan's story checked out. Nancy asked Sergeant Weinberg, "May I go in?"

"Be my guest," he said. "Everyone else stay on the path. I'm going to check for footprints. Though with the dry weather we've had this past week, I doubt we'll find any. Andy," he said to his partner, "go get the fingerprint kit from the car. Let's dust the shed for prints."

"You'll find mine." Bryan sounded nervous again. Nancy motioned Ned to stay outside. She stepped through the doorway, careful not to touch anything. Except for a few plastic bags of fertilizer, the shed was empty.

"Is the door usually locked?" she asked, rejoining the others.

"Yes," Dr. Morrison answered for Bryan. "Even though there's nothing valuable inside, we don't want students hanging out on museum property."

"The thief probably knew Bryan's routine," said Nancy. "And he—or she—had cased out the museum facilities like the shed."

"Considering the thief made off with the most valuable painting in the collection, I'd say this was the work of a pro," Dr. Morrison added.

Bryan's eyes went wide. "You mean Jared's *First Kiss*? They stole that?" Bryan looked at Debbie for confirmation.

Nancy followed his glance. Debbie was hovering near the wall of the storeroom. She nodded bleakly. "The one I showed you yesterday after hanging the show."

"Bryan, how do you get past the security system?" Nancy inquired.

"With this." Bryan fished a little plastic card out of his pocket. "It deactivates the system."

"The system was off," Dean Jarvis explained to Bryan.

"Not when I made my last rounds," Bryan said firmly. "The security company will vouch for that. Whoever turned off the alarm and opened that window did it after I was locked in the shed."

Dr. Morrison broke in. "When you were in the storage room checking the inventory, Debbie, did you open the window?"

Debbie was so pale Nancy was sure she would faint. "I don't remember—really."

"We'll check the storeroom for prints, too," said the sergeant, taking the fingerprint kit from his partner and starting for the shed.

"Why bother with the storeroom window?" asked George. "Isn't it too small to get a painting through?"

"The painting's small, too." Debbie sounded weak. "It's only nine by twelve inches."

So they couldn't rule out escape through the storeroom, Nancy realized. That meant Debbie really could have been involved. The window was tiny, but so was Debbie. Though in that suit she could scarcely scale a wall to the skylight. She could have handed the painting to someone outside, though. Bryan? But why bother with breaking the skylight and going through windows, if Debbie could get in and out of the museum by turning off the security system?

"If you don't need me," Dr. Morrison said, "I should put in a call to the insurance company."

"I'll come with you, Geoff," Dean Jarvis said.

"Debbie, I want to speak with you inside." Dr. Morrison's tone was curt.

"Things don't look too good for her," murmured George, so only Nancy could hear. Nancy nodded. George had worked with Nancy on enough cases to know that everyone was a suspect until the real culprit was found. So far the evidence was strongly pointing to Debbie—with or without an accomplice.

Nancy tried to organize her thoughts. "The roof," she said out loud. "Sergeant Weinberg, okay if we check out the roof?"

"Sure, Nancy. Just keep me posted."

Nancy motioned Bryan to join their search of the roof. "You know the building, so you might spot something that we'd miss."

A moment later they had ascended the narrow

staircase leading from the back hall of the museum to the emergency exit on the roof.

The tarred flat roof was littered with branches, twigs, and other debris. Nancy stooped down to inspect the broken skylight. Glass shards jutted out from the edge of the frame, the points glittering in the moonlight. Bryan aimed his flashlight on the skylight. "Don't touch anything," Nancy warned. "There might be prints, and that glass looks dangerous."

Lying beside the window were some climbing gear and a hammer. Using a tissue, Nancy gingerly picked up the hammer, careful not to smudge any potential prints. George identified it as a climbing hammer, used to scale rock walls.

Nancy reached down through the skylight with it and was just able to snare the rope. She lifted it up and into the beam of their flashlight.

As the climbing line came into view, Bryan caught his breath. Nancy turned around. Bryan looked shocked—but only for a moment.

"Is something wrong?" Nancy asked.

"No, nothing. It's just that it's a new rope," Bryan said casually. "I'm surprised someone left it and the other stuff behind."

"Maybe Dean Jarvis and Dr. Morrison arrived just as the thief was making his getaway. He'd have to leave the gear then," George suggested. "It's pretty expensive to replace, though."

Nancy rested the rope on the edge of the skylight and shifted back on her heels. She noticed a small scrap of paper she hadn't seen before. It was a ticket stub from a campus concert given by the rock group EC, Environmental Confusion, the Friday night before.

"Ned," she began thoughtfully, "have you had any very windy days since Friday?"

Ned laughed. "No way. It's been dead calm."

She showed Ned the ticket stub. "How would this blow up on the roof with no wind?" she asked.

"Maybe the thief dropped the ticket," George suggested.

"Just what I'm thinking." Then she added cautiously, "Or a worker who had reason to be on the roof."

"Still, it's something," Ned said.

"We'd better tell the sergeant what we found. He'll bag the evidence and dust for prints later. Actually we've gotten some pretty good leads," Nancy said. "The ticket stub, the climbing apparatus, the new rope."

When the group returned to the entrance hall, they found Dr. Morrison confronting Debbie, whose face had gone from pale to beet red. "I can't believe you're firing me. It's not fair. I didn't steal the painting."

"That's not the point. You were working late without permission. You forgot to reset the alarm. The thieves probably got in from the roof, not the storeroom, but you did leave that storeroom window open. Until this is cleared up I don't want you in this museum. So get your things and leave now, please."

Debbie glared up at him, then turned and stormed down the hall to her office.

Nancy felt sorry for the girl.

Sergeant Weinberg came up to Bryan and asked him to retrace the route of his security rounds. Before Bryan left he asked Ned to wait for Debbie and walk her back to the Theta Pi house. "She doesn't have a car here and it's pretty late."

"No problem," said Ned.

Soon Debbie returned carrying a cardboard box. Her cheeks were streaked with tears, but she held her head high as she marched past Dr. Morrison. The foursome walked out of the museum and headed for Greek Row.

They had just reached the Theta Pi house when a beat-up green sedan screeched up the drive, heading for the sorority parking area.

"Whoa, who's that driving?" Nancy asked.

"Rina O'Neill," Debbie answered, and a second later a slender girl in black leggings and a black sleeveless tunic came around the side of the house. She wore a black beret pulled down at an extreme angle over her long red hair.

"Hey, Rina, how's it going?" Ned called out as he put Debbie's box down on the top step of the porch.

Keys in hand, the girl strode past them all without answering. She completely ignored Ned but managed to glare at Debbie. She unlocked the front door of the sorority house, walked in, and slammed the door hard behind her.

"What was that about?" Nancy asked.

Debbie plopped down next to her box. "Rina's got it in for me for a couple of reasons. She used to be Bryan's girlfriend—in high school—and then Bryan and I started dating over the summer, and now . . ."

"She blames you for breaking them up," George supplied knowingly.

"Not that things are that great with me and Bryan, either. . . ." Debbie's voice trailed off. "He's a great guy, but we don't have that much in common." She made a tripod with her elbows on her knees and dropped her chin into her hands as she stared across the broad tree-lined street. A moment later she continued. "He's the outdoorsy type. I'm more a museum person. While Bryan rock-climbed this summer, I taught art history at the McKinleyville halfway house for runaways—"

"You teach runaways?" Nancy's impression of Debbie changed as Debbie told them about teaching high school kids. Debbie became animated, sure of herself, and not at all like the scared little girl Nancy had glimpsed back at the museum.

"Maybe that's what you should do when you graduate," Ned suggested. "Instead of being a curator."

Debbie's smile flickered out. "As if I have a choice now," she said bitterly. "No museum is going to hire a person who's been within a light-year of an art heist."

Debbie stopped talking, and the foursome sat

in silence a moment. Finally Nancy spoke up. "Debbie," she said, "you mentioned Rina was angry with you for a couple of reasons. Bryan was one. What's the other?"

Debbie leaned back against a porch pillar. "Rina didn't win the Emerson art contest. I was one of the judges—Dr. Morrison and Michael Jared were the others."

Nancy thoughtfully chewed on her lower lip as Debbie went on. "I've heard about how you helped the Theta Pis before. Please help me. If you don't clear my name, my career will be over. Please find that painting."

"I'm sure going to try," Nancy said. "If you remember something—no matter how silly it may seem—about tonight or about the painting, let me know."

"I will." Debbie rose, shoving her hands into the deep pockets of her silk suit jacket. "But I had nothing to do with the theft. You have to believe that."

"I'll do my best to solve this mystery" was all Nancy could promise.

George picked up Debbie's box and followed her inside, saying she was ready for bed. As the door closed behind them, Ned took Nancy's hand and tugged her down the steps. "Where are we going?" Nancy whispered, not quite sure what Ned had up his sleeve.

"Remember—this is supposed to be *our* fun weekend," he said. "And just because mysteries have a nutty way of tracking you down, that doesn't mean I'm going to lose out on the fun part. A pig-out at I Screams counts as fun—no?"

"Definitely!" Nancy lifted herself up on her toes to kiss him. They held each other a minute, then drew apart. Nancy searched Ned's eyes. All she saw was love. Still, she was worried. George's warning about taking Ned for granted had struck a nerve.

"Ned, how do you feel about my detective work?" Nancy asked as they turned the corner of Greek Row onto Emersonville's main commercial street.

Ned waited until they were in line at the ice-cream counter before he answered. "I could say I don't care. Or that I think it's great—because part of me does—really."

"But it bothers you," Nancy realized as they moved up in the line. "You're disappointed I took on this case."

His shoulders tensed up slightly. "Yes, I guess I am. I thought for once we'd have a weekend together without your running off every five seconds checking out some clue—" Ned shrugged, heaved a sigh, and looked down at Nancy.

"Oh, Ned. I'm sorry. I just didn't know how to turn it down."

"I know." Ned stepped up to the counter and ordered. He handed Nancy her frozen yogurt and grinned. "Let's just enjoy what time we do have." As they headed back past the stately houses on Greek Row, he draped his free arm over her shoulder. "I guess it's my luck to have fallen for a girl who's got a really crazy talent for solving mysteries. It's probably part of why I love you."

Nancy didn't hear what he said next. She leaned into his chest and gave a contented sigh. Ned had said the magic words. He did love her, and she loved him. What else mattered?

Nancy woke up with a jolt. For a moment she had no idea where she was. The sound of someone breathing across the room jarred her memory. It's Ned's fraternity party weekend. That's Chris Harper in the other bed, and I'm sharing her room. Nancy plumped up her pillow and closed her eyes to go back to sleep. She was startled wide awake by a noise.

Out of bed in a flash, Nancy tiptoed to the window, trying not to wake Chris. Looking out, she saw a shadowy female figure throwing pebbles at the house. It was probably a sorority sister locked out. After groping in the dark for her lightweight robe, Nancy threw it on over her T-shirt and headed downstairs.

She crept quietly past the original cook's room, which was now a bedroom, and noticed the light was on in there. When she reached the back door and opened it, the yard was empty. "Hello?" she called out softly. Nancy heard nothing except the chirp of crickets.

She looked up to the second floor. All the bedrooms were dark. Where had the girl gone?

Back inside, Nancy knocked at the door of the ground-floor bedroom. After a minute Debbie answered. "Nancy? What's up?"

"I saw someone in the yard. She was throwing pebbles at the house—I figured at your window. Was someone locked out?"

"No," Debbie replied curtly. "I'd have heard—I've been up reading." Debbie began to close the door in Nancy's face. "Look, it's late. I've got to get some rest, it's been an awful night."

Before Nancy could respond, Debbie closed the door firmly.

Nancy was wide awake now. Quickly she sorted through the facts. If Debbie was awake, she had to have heard the pebbles hitting the house.

Why was she lying, and what had happened to the girl in the yard?

Chapter

Three

"READY?" George asked, poking her head into Nancy's room the next morning. Nancy was at the mirror, touching up her makeup before breakfast.

"Almost." Nancy returned George's smile in the mirror. "You look great!"

George was wearing khaki shorts and a peach halter top that set off her creamy complexion. Nancy had chosen a short denim skirt and a pink tank top.

"Thanks. You, too," said George.

As Nancy dabbed on lip gloss, she told George about the mysterious visitor the night before.

"Debbie's hiding something for sure," George agreed. "But right now I don't care. I'm starving. Let's eat."

Downstairs, Brook Albright, Rosie Lopez, and

a couple of other sorority sisters Nancy knew from previous visits to Emerson were already at the huge dining room table.

"Over here!" Chris Harper, Nancy's roommate, yelled. "I saved you a couple of seats."

Nancy grinned back at the tall dark-haired girl. "Great. Did you remember to save some of those famous Theta Pi biscuits for George?"

"The only reason I tagged along," quipped George.

Chris laughed. "Don't say that so loud. The Omega Chi guys think you came for them and the party tonight."

"Forget the boys, stick to the biscuits," Brook joked with a toss of her wavy auburn hair. "More predictable." She introduced herself to George and asked Nancy, "What brings you to Emerson this time?"

"Another case?" Rosie asked, pulling in her chair so Nancy and George could pass by and get to the sideboard. Nancy poured herself some coffee and selected a muffin from one of the serving plates.

"Yes and no," Nancy said. "I came for the Roaring Twenties party at Omega Chi."

"But her plans changed," George said, heaping her plate with sausage and biscuits.

"Don't tell me," Brook gasped. She tapped the copy of the local morning paper lying open beside her on the table. "The museum robbery."

"And you're already in the middle of it." Rosie sounded impressed.

"Guess I missed the scoop. I was asleep before you got in last night." Chris slid her chair down to make more room for Nancy.

Nancy sipped her coffee. "What's the paper say?"

Brook frowned. "That a painting called *First Kiss* was stolen last night. But there aren't any pictures of the painting. Only of the gorgeous painter. Not that I'm complaining."

Nancy and George laughed.

"Do you think Debbie knows about the robbery?" asked Rosie, biting into a muffin. "The Jared exhibit was Debbie's special project."

At that moment Nancy heard footsteps behind her. Turning, she saw Debbie walk in, another sorority sister, Trish Hardcastle, following on her heels. To Nancy, Debbie looked exhausted. Her face was pale and drawn, and dark circles bruised the skin below her eyes.

"Did you know the museum was robbed, Debbie?" Brook asked.

"Yes," Debbie said quietly. She took a plate and got in line at the sideboard.

From her seat at the table Nancy observed Debbie closely. She was surprised by how much food the petite girl heaped on her plate.

"Why, Debbie, I guess stress really perks up your appetite," a cool voice said from the doorway.

Debbie's whole body stiffened. Brook and Rosie exchanged a glance. Nancy turned around.

Rina was propped against the doorframe. She was dressed in skintight black leggings and a black tank top, and she was holding a large art portfolio at her side.

"I heard about the robbery, Deb. Too bad." Rina strode into the dining room and grabbed an apple from the bowl of fruit on the table. "But I guess it was about time your luck ran out."

"Rina!" Chris warned.

Rina gave a careless shrug and wandered out of the room. A moment later the front door slammed after her.

Debbie smiled wanly. "I'm not feeling well," she said. "I think I'll eat in my room." She hurried off.

"Big appetite for a sick person," George whispered to Nancy. Nancy nodded. She thought about the mysterious visitor of the night before and wondered if Debbie had had a guest for breakfast this morning.

"Rina's really getting out of hand," Trish said, tossing back her blond pigtail.

"Just be patient," Brook responded. "Rina's having a tough time right now. She hasn't paid all her tuition money and I know she's scared to death. The school won't wait forever for it."

"Rina works super hard, too," Chris said. "She has two jobs, plus classes. It doesn't leave her much time for fun."

"Lots of us have jobs," Trish countered defensively. "And, yeah, maybe her job with the food

29

service is tough, but ushering? That's hardly even a job. Last week when we were all scrambling for EC tickets, Rina got into the concert for free."

"Whoa!" Rosie protested. "I will personally testify that ushering can be hard work. Last night Rina and I ushered at this terrible experimental play. It went on forever and was boring."

"Not to change the subject or anything," Chris said, clearing her throat. "But what are you guys wearing to the party tonight?"

"Nancy rented outrageous twenties dresses for both of us," George said.

"I heard from Trish that Debbie's got the most beautiful green sequined dress," Brook informed them. "Trish says she's bound to win the best costume award."

"That would be great—she needs something to cheer her up," Chris said.

"Really," Rosie remarked. "She's been talking about breaking up with Bryan lately."

"Not her type, if you ask me," Trish said. "Too much of a jock—she needs someone artsy—"

"Like Michael Jared." Four girls giggled at once.

Nancy only half-listened to the girls' conversation, her mind on the case. Something about Debbie was not on the up-and-up. Nancy needed to talk to her more to figure out what.

After breakfast Nancy headed straight for Debbie's room. She knocked on the door. Leaning close, she heard shuffling noises inside, and then the door opened a crack. Debbie blocked Nancy's view of the room.

"May I come in?" Nancy asked. "I have some questions."

Debbie hesitated, then opened the door. Nancy walked in and took a quick glance around. Debbie appeared to be alone. The L-shaped room had a bunk bed, two desks and bureaus, and a tall oak bookcase. The pale peach walls were covered with artwork. Through the open window Nancy could smell the flowers in the backyard. Then she noticed the empty plate on one of the desks. "Feeling better?" she asked.

Debbie seemed confused.

"You ate all your breakfast."

Debbie drew in her breath and fiddled with some bottles on her dresser. "You said you had some questions," she answered, avoiding Nancy's eyes.

Nancy began the conversation carefully. "Did you paint this?" Nancy pointed to a watercolor of running horses on the wall.

Debbie shook her head. "Not me. I don't paint. One of the girls at the halfway house painted that."

"This, too?" Nancy stood in front of a child-like drawing of a farmhouse.

"No. That's Rina's."

Nancy couldn't keep the look of surprise off her face. Rina seemed much too sophisticated to paint such a simple scene.

Debbie must have read her expression. "It's her latest style. Rina's always trying out new styles."

Nancy walked to the far corner of the room. "The *Mona Lisa*," she said in surprise.

"My roommate Kate made that copy this summer as an assignment for an art course she's taking in Paris," Debbie told her. "She sent it to me for my birthday. She's a wonderful artist."

"I don't think I've met Kate on my other trips to Emerson," Nancy said. "Where is she?"

"Still in Paris—until next week."

"But what about her classes?"

"I enrolled Kate, and she wrote to her teachers telling them she'd be late. Her registration packet is in her desk."

Nancy took a closer look at the painting. "Kate's copy looks so much like the original—except that it's smaller, I think."

"That's right," Debbie said. "No one's allowed to copy the art the exact size as the original. Otherwise, the copy might be passed off as an original. And that would be forgery."

"That's odd, isn't it. I mean the distinction between a copy and a forgery."

"A copy is a forgery only when there's the intent to deceive." Debbie sounded bored. "Now, Nancy, if you don't have any more questions—"

"Just a couple of things about the robbery. Really, I won't take long." Nancy took a seat on the bottom bunk. Debbie leaned against the closet.

"How long have you been assistant curator?"

"Six months."

"And Bryan? How long has he been a guard?"

"I hired Bryan right after I was appointed," Debbie replied. "Rina suggested him for the job. In fact, she gave me that painting as a thank-you present for hiring him." Debbie glanced at Rina's painting. Nancy couldn't read Debbie's expression.

"So Bryan and Rina split up after you two began working together," Nancy said thoughtfully.

"Yes," said Debbie. "As I told you last night, we started dating this summer, which got Rina upset." Debbie eyed Nancy nervously. "I don't understand what these questions have to do with the theft of *First Kiss.*"

Nancy wasn't sure, either. All she knew was that Debbie was a suspect, as was Bryan. Both had opportunity. Nancy had no more questions for Debbie just then. She thanked her and left to find George.

George was outside on the veranda fanning herself with the newspaper. Nancy suggested that they drop by the art museum to find out if there was any word on *First Kiss.* In the museum parking lot Nancy spotted the black sports car from the night before—its license plates read MORRISON.

The two girls strolled into the Jared gallery, and Nancy saw that Dr. Morrison was not alone. A young man dressed in black jeans and a black T-shirt was talking agitatedly with the curator. He kept running his hands through his short black hair as he focused on the blank space on the wall.

"That's him. That's Michael Jared with Dr. Morrison," Nancy whispered as she pulled George back into the foyer.

"What a hunk," George said, peering around the corner.

Nancy giggled behind her hand. "You sound like Bess."

George pretended to be offended. "I'm just stating a fact. If Bess were here she'd have fainted, not spoken."

As Nancy moved into the gallery, Dr. Morrison spotted her. "Ah, Michael, here's someone you should meet." He motioned Nancy over to him. George followed. "This is Nancy Drew and her friend George Fayne."

Michael stared first at Nancy, then at George and then back at Nancy again. His clear blue eyes seemed to bore right through her. "Michael Jared here," he said, putting out his hand.

Nancy shook it. She realized he was probably twenty-five or six, but he could have passed for one of Ned's classmates, even up close.

"I'm sorry about your painting, Mr. Jared," Nancy said. "Dean Jarvis asked me to help with the investigation—"

Michael Jared's thick eyebrows arched up and he stared harder at Nancy. Dr. Morrison cleared his throat. "Actually Ms. Drew here is quite a detective. Both the police and the dean have used her before to solve mysteries on campus."

The dark-haired artist's expression shifted from confusion to respect. "Really? I assumed you were a student here." He folded his arms across his chest. Nancy noticed he had a small rose tattooed on his right bicep. "I really appreciate your help. Any leads yet?"

Nancy shook her head. "It's a bit early for anything yet, Mr. Jared."

"Michael," he corrected with a quick grin. It was such a disarming smile, Nancy had to smile back. "All this mister stuff makes me feel so old."

"Dr. Morrison, you have a call on line two," a female voice announced over the museum intercom. The curator excused himself. "Probably the insurance company," he muttered.

Nancy pulled a small notebook and pencil out of her backpack. "I wonder if you could tell me something about the painting—why someone would steal that particular one."

Michael shook his head ruefully. "Hard to say really. It is *my* favorite and one critic did call it one of my strongest." He looked back at the empty space on the wall, and his expression was so wistful Nancy's heart ached for him. "But then the same critic called that landscape over there a near masterpiece." He sounded proud and a little embarrassed. "They could have taken that."

"No," George spoke up firmly. "It's too big. The thief had to fit it out the skylight *or* the storeroom window. *First Kiss* was smaller."

"So that's how they broke in," the artist said, looking up at the skylight, which was already neatly boarded up. Nancy and George began to fill Michael in on the details of the robbery as they knew them.

He listened attentively to George, but kept catching Nancy's eye. Michael finally turned directly to Nancy. "Sorry to keep staring at you, but I love your coloring."

George's eyes went wide, and Nancy felt self-conscious all at once.

Michael laughed. "I didn't mean to embarrass you. I need a costumed model to pose for my class this afternoon. My usual model is about your size and has strawberry blond hair like yours. This morning she called in sick. With all this commotion over the painting I haven't had time to find anyone else. Would you consider posing for the class?

"Me, pose?" Had Michael Jared actually asked *her* to pose for him?

"Oh, Nancy, do it!" George urged, her dark eyes shining. "You'll hang in a museum."

"You mean my *picture* may hang in a museum," Nancy said. "And I doubt a student's work would end up in a museum, but"—she

turned to Michael and regarded him thoughtfully—"okay. I'd be honored."

After Michael told her the place and time for
his class, she excused herself. "Dr. Morrison is
probably off the phone by now, and I want to get
a photo of the missing painting from him."

The receptionist told Nancy where to find Dr.
Morrison. Nancy headed down a long tiled hall-
way lined with offices and closets.

As Nancy approached Dr. Morrison's office,
she noticed the door was open. She could hear
that he was still on the phone, so she slowed
down. She didn't want to interrupt his phone
call. Without warning his voice rose, its tone
desperate, almost shrill.

"I know I'm late," Dr. Morrison was saying.
Nancy crept closer to the open door. Dr. Morrison fell silent a moment. "No. I am not backing
out of it. Not at all." His tone was still loud and
desperate but very firm.

"I'll get the money," he said. "Soon."

Chapter

Four

THE RECEIVER WAS SLAMMED DOWN. Nancy stepped back quickly. Was Dr. Morrison in debt? Was he being blackmailed?

The curator stormed out of his office, almost crashing into Nancy. "What are you doing here?"

"I wanted to ask you something," Nancy replied.

Dr. Morrison took a deep breath. "Yes, Nancy, of course. Sorry I'm so jumpy—the theft and all. Make yourself comfortable. I'll be right back."

Inside the office a group of photographs on one wall caught Nancy's eye. They were all of Dr. Morrison in various exotic locales. There was also a photo of a new colonial-style mansion. Pretty pricey place for a curator on a college payroll, Nancy mused. She heard Dr. Morrison approaching and turned around.

She greeted him with a smile. "Yours?" Nancy pointed to the picture of the mansion.

"My wife and I just built it outside of town."

"Lovely," Nancy said quietly, but her thoughts were racing. "I'll get the money. Soon." Those were his exact words on the phone. Then Nancy remembered that unlike Debbie or Bryan, the curator had an airtight alibi. He'd been at dinner with the dean when the museum was burgled. Unless he had an accomplice, Dr. Morrison had to be in the clear.

"Was there something you wanted, Nancy?"

"Do you have a photograph of *First Kiss*?"

Dr. Morrison extracted a small color print from a bulging file on his cluttered desk.

Nancy caught her breath as she gazed at the photograph. The painting was of a young couple. The boy's head was turned away from the viewer, but the girl's face was clearly visible. She was blond and very young and was looking up at the boy. On her face was an expression of yearning, tinged with vulnerability. The artist had exactly captured the moment before a girl's first kiss.

Nancy studied the photo a moment, then slipped it into her notebook. "Do you have any ideas who might have stolen the painting?"

He met her gaze straight on. "I don't *know* anything. And I certainly don't want to place any blame on anyone, but"—he hesitated a moment—"Debbie certainly had no reason to be here last night." He held up a hand to ward off Nancy's comment. "I know—the inventory—but that could have waited until today. And as for Bryan—well, do you buy that story about his being locked in a shed? *And* he's a rock climber."

Before she could respond, a rangy middle-aged man wearing green overalls stuck his head through the doorway. "I finished boarding up the skylight. The glass company will be out tomorrow," he said.

"This is Ralph Jenkins, our maintenance man," Dr. Morrison said. "Nancy is helping with the investigation," he explained.

Nancy smiled. "I'd like to ask you a few questions."

"Yeah?" Jenkins replied brusquely.

She ignored his rudeness. "On the roof last night," she began, "I found a ticket to last Friday's EC concert. I wondered if you might have dropped it."

"I don't go to rock concerts," Jenkins snapped.

"Or if you knew of anyone else who'd been up to the roof recently," Nancy continued pleasantly.

"Hasn't been anyone up on the roof," Jenkins growled, "until last night, that is." Muttering under his breath, he left the room.

Why was Jenkins so hostile? "How long has Mr. Jenkins worked at the museum?" she asked.

"One year. I brought Ralph with me from the Cabbott Museum in Chicago."

"Isn't it unusual for a maintenance person to follow a curator?"

"Perhaps." Dr. Morrison laughed lightly. "But Ralph is a good man. I trust him."

"Why did you come to Emerson from the Cabbott?" Nancy asked. "The Cabbott is such a prestigious museum with a wonderful collection."

"You are quite the detective, Nancy," he said. "Am I a suspect now?"

Nancy returned the curator's smile.

"I came to Emerson for a number of reasons," he finally answered. "Mainly for the quiet small-town lifestyle but also for the freedom to exhibit more experimental art."

"Will the theft be very damaging?"

Removing his glasses, Dr. Morrison rubbed his eyes. "Yes, it's going to hurt us. People won't contribute money or paintings to a museum with poor security. Traveling exhibits will be canceled. The college and Emerson students will suffer in the end. That's why it's crucial to find the thief," Dr. Morrison added fiercely.

"I'll do my best," Nancy promised.

George was waiting for her in the lobby. "I'd like to check out the sporting goods stores near campus," Nancy said. "I want to find out if that climbing rope used in the robbery was bought recently. I have a hunch that our thief is here on campus and bought the rope nearby."

* * *

After a morning of inquiries, Nancy and George rested by dangling their feet in the cool water of the quad fountain as they waited for Ned. The open space in front of the student union was crowded with students.

A girl in pink overalls skated up and handed George a flyer. "Hey, Nan, this must be my lucky day. This flyer entitles me to a free makeover at the beauty school at the corner of Emerson and Main."

Nancy elbowed George in the ribs. "Bess always tells us blonds have more fun," Nancy teased, refering to George's cousin. "Go for it."

George laughed, then pointed in the direction of the ivy-covered administration building across the quad. "Hey, there's Debbie. With a tall, skinny girl in a red shirt." Nancy looked over. Debbie's friend had long brown hair and a small, pointy face. Neither of them looked too happy. A moment later Nancy lost sight of them in the crowd.

The clock struck twelve-thirty. Stepping up onto the fountain wall, Nancy looked around the plaza. She spied a familiar figure in jeans and a T-shirt loping through the crowd. "Ned!"

Ned's arm shot up into the air as he quickened his pace, swerving around some girls on skates.

Nancy punched him playfully when he hugged her. "You're late, Nickerson," she told him.

Ned grinned. "Sorry, but my chemistry professor kept us after class." Ned eased himself down onto the edge of the fountain. "How's the investigation?"

"Hard to tell," Nancy said. "We learned that three people bought climbing rope at a store near campus in the last month, all with credit cards."

"But the store won't release the buyers' names to Nancy," George added.

"I can't reach Sergeant Weinberg," Nancy explained. "I'll have to get the buyers' names from him. I'll try him later."

"Sounds frustrating," Ned said sympathetically.

"We also stopped at the box office," Nancy continued. "There's no way to find out who bought that particular concert ticket. Strictly general admission."

"Maybe I'm your thief," Ned said, pretending to rummage in his pocket. "I can't find my stub."

"Right, Nickerson," Nancy quipped. "But I'm your alibi for yesterday." She snuggled closer to him. Ned was just as much a hunk as Michael Jared. Even hunkier. "We also stopped at a gallery on Main Street and showed the owner a photo of *First Kiss*—in case the thief was an amateur who might try to sell the painting in town. No luck."

Out of the corner of her eye, Nancy noticed Bryan Barbour trudging down the student union steps. Ned saw him, too, and waved Bryan over. "What's up?" Ned asked as he walked over.

Bryan shrugged. "Debbie was going to meet me at eleven-thirty, but she didn't show up."

"We just saw her," Nancy said.

"Yeah?" Bryan sighed. "I guess I've been stood up. She probably blames me for the break-in and her losing her job."

"Come on," Ned said. "No one blames you."

But you're still a suspect, Nancy said to herself. We've only got your word about being locked in the shed.

"Why don't you have lunch with us?" George suggested.

Bryan lit up. "I could do that."

"Let's try the new Art Café in the union."

Bryan made a face at Ned's suggestion.

"Is there a problem with the café?" Nancy asked.

"No." Bryan shrugged. "The café's fine."

They walked down the ramp that cut through the center of the union and then took the stairs to the second floor. The Art Café was a dark cavelike room with walls covered with paintings.

Nancy spotted the reason for Bryan's hesitation: Rina. She was working behind the counter.

As they filed past Rina with their trays, Bryan smiled tentatively at her. Rina didn't smile back.

"Nice seeing you, too, Rina," Bryan muttered as he took his sandwich. With cool efficiency, Rina served Nancy next.

"Does anyone mind if we eat outside?" Bryan asked after they'd paid for their food. "It's a little tense in here." The others agreed and made their way back down the stairs.

When they reached the lobby Nancy said, "I'll

meet you guys outside." She wanted to try Sergeant Weinberg again. Several phones were free, but Nancy had no change. Frustrated, she ran into the bookstore.

The line at the cash register snaked ten deep down a narrow aisle, made narrower by bins full of art supplies lining the space. A supply list for Michael Jared's painting class was posted over one bin. Nancy looked in, curious. She saw small shrink-wrapped packages labeled "Jared—Art Starter Kit" with the course number printed on the outside.

"Pardon me," a soft voice said as the line inched forward. Nancy let a tall girl with a red shirt squeeze past. She looked familiar. Of course, Nancy thought—the girl was Debbie's friend, the one George had spied across the quad earlier. Nancy craned her neck looking for Debbie, but she didn't see her.

The girl was in front of the art supply bins. After a quick check over her shoulder, she slipped a Jared class packet into her backpack and calmly walked out of the store.

Debbie's friend a shoplifter? Nancy forgot about her change and rushed outside after the girl.

Chapter

Five

THE SUN BLINDED NANCY long enough for the girl to put some distance between them. She must have sensed that someone was watching her, because she suddenly took off, losing herself in the crowd. Nancy ran after her.

Just then a horde of shouting, sweaty guys in shorts, T-shirts, and headbands charged across Nancy's path.

"Watch out, babe!" one of the guys yelled.

Nancy circled around the pack of athletes, but by the time she was in the clear, the girl was gone.

Nancy sighed. She wondered whether Debbie would be willing to identify the girl. Feeling frustrated, Nancy joined her friends.

Ned was finishing his sandwich, and George

was almost through with her shrimp salad. Bryan's plate was totally clean.

"Where have you been?" Ned asked, concerned.

"Don't ask," Nancy said. "I never did get to call Sergeant Weinberg." She described what had happened. "I'm sure it was Debbie's friend." Turning to Bryan, she asked, "Does she sound like someone you might have met?"

"Not really."

Nancy was finishing up her salad when Michael Jared approached their outdoor table. Her stomach flipped over once.

Nancy blushed slightly as Michael walked up, his eyes fixed on hers.

"Hi, Nancy. George." He turned back to Nancy. "Anything happening?"

"Nothing yet," Nancy said. Then she remembered Michael hadn't met Ned or Bryan. She introduced them.

"Sorry about your painting," Ned said, shaking Jared's hand. Nancy frowned. She detected a note of something—annoyance, jealousy, in Ned's voice.

"Thanks, man," Michael said. Then he smiled again at Nancy. "So I'll expect you at the studio at a quarter to three. You'll need a few minutes to change for the modeling session." He took off for the exit.

"Modeling session?" Ned stared at Nancy. "I don't get it, Nan. First you agree to help Dean

Jarvis with this case. Then you decide to book whatever free time you have by posing for Jared." Ned crumpled his napkin and tossed it onto his tray. "Exactly when do *we* see each other?"

Nancy couldn't believe the hurt in his eyes. "Ned," she cried, "we couldn't be together this afternoon, anyway. You have classes. Besides, it'll give me a chance to talk to Michael."

"I'm sure it will," Ned snapped.

Nancy's mouth fell open. "You're jealous."

"Shouldn't I be?" Ned said, pushing his chair back from the table. "You came here to spend time with me. But everything and everyone else has gotten top priority."

Ned tossed his paper plate into a wastebasket and grabbed his backpack. "See you guys later."

Nancy stared forlornly after Ned as he vanished into the crowd. George patted Nancy's hand, then focused on Bryan. Nancy felt awful. She had just had a pretty serious fight with Ned in front of their friends.

Nancy picked at her salad as she listened to Bryan tell George about a climbing trip he planned the next weekend to Indian Rock State Park. After a few minutes he started to talk about the theft.

"What a bum deal for Mr. Jared. He's a good guy." Bryan twisted his gold earring. "But art collectors will do anything to get a painting they want. I know this one collector named Ian Sanders—I crewed on his yacht in the Caribbean." Bryan tilted his chair back. "Now, there's the life. I sure would give anything to be that rich," he said dreamily, then shook his head. "What am I talking about? I'll never have that kind of dough."

Nancy leaned forward and listened carefully as Bryan continued to describe Ian Sanders's lifestyle. "He spent a million bucks for some little painting last year, just because he loved it."

"Ian Sanders," George mused. "That name is familiar."

"Ian's name is in the paper whenever there's a bidding war on some famous painting," Bryan said. "In fact, he happens to be crazy about Jared's stuff and is coming to Emerson for the opening. He's taking me to dinner Monday night."

Bryan pulled a pair of black in-line skates out of his backpack. "I'd better hit the road." He stuffed his red hightops into his pack, changed into the skates, then turned to George shyly.

"Nancy's modeling at three. Are you busy?"

George cocked her head. "No—not really."

"I was heading over to the Climbing Wall— that's a climbing gym in town. Ever climbed before?"

"Sure. I love it," George said. "If Nancy doesn't need me, I'd love to come with you. It'll be fun."

"Great idea," said Nancy. "Let's call Sergeant Weinberg now and see what he's found out."

George and Bryan set up a meeting place, then

Bryan skated off across the quad. Nancy and George went in to the bank of telephones in the union lobby.

Sergeant Weinberg was on another line so Nancy left a message that she'd call back in a couple of minutes. Then she phoned her father, Carson Drew, because she needed information on Dr. Morrison. She was hoping her dad knew someone connected with Chicago's Cabbott Museum who could help them understand Morrison's need for money. Reaching her father, Nancy briefed him on the case.

"I do know someone on the Cabbott board of directors," he said. "I'll find out what I can. But I want you to be careful, Nancy."

"I will, Dad. Give my love to Hannah," Nancy added, including the woman who'd been their housekeeper for the past fifteen years.

Nancy tried Sergeant Weinberg again, and this time reached him. "I got your message," the sergeant said. "And I have those names for you."

Nancy copied down the names and telephone numbers of the three people who had purchased rope at Outdoors Unlimited in the last month— Arnold Salomon, Michelle Vasquez, and Bryan Barbour. "Bryan?" Nancy repeated.

"That surprised me, too," the sergeant admitted. "It's probably just a coincidence, but since Bryan was at the scene of the crime, I'd like to know where his rope is."

"I'll find out," Nancy assured him.

"If you'd check on all three purchasers, it

would sure help me out, Nancy. I'm jammed up right now. Oh, by the way. The hammer and jumars were wiped clean of prints. If we're dealing with an amateur, it's a clever amateur."

After Nancy filled George in on her talk with Sergeant Weinberg, George's face fell. "I wish you could rule out Bryan."

"Everyone's a suspect," Nancy reminded her. George nodded sadly. "I know. I just don't want to believe he's guilty."

"You're starting to like him."

"I can't help it. And I don't think he's really serious about Debbie either."

"She's just about ready to give up on him, too," Nancy said. "But he's not free yet, George."

George gave a quick smile. "All I'm doing is going climbing with him. And it's going to stay that way unless they really break up." George leaned against the wall. "But he *is* cute, and fun, and—I don't think he's your thief, Nancy."

"I hope not, but meanwhile, I need your help, George. This afternoon at the climbing gym, try to find out if Bryan still has his climbing rope. I'll check with the other people Weinberg mentioned, Michelle Vasquez and Mr. Salomon."

"Okay," George said, resigned. "But I bet you're wrong about Bryan."

"Me, too," Nancy admitted.

"Oh, I almost forgot." George handed Nancy a slip of paper. "There are two more art galleries and one more sporting goods store—called

Marshalls—in town," George said. "And, by the way, Bryan gave me this information," she added pointedly, and left.

Nancy spent the next hour following up on Michelle Vasquez and Mr. Salomon. Unfortunately for Bryan, she was able to cross them both off her list of suspects. Both had had the store send the rope as gifts to people out of town.

Glancing at her watch, she saw that it was almost three and had to race over to the art building. She felt a little nervous because she had never modeled before.

Michael met her at the studio door, holding a small unfinished painting. "Hello, there!" He flashed Nancy a quick smile.

Nancy's heart was pounding as Michael led her down a narrow hall to a dressing room. The artist took a hanger off the rack and handed a gypsy costume to Nancy.

Jared propped the painting he had brought with him up against the mirror. "Try to fix your hair as close as possible to the model's in this painting."

"I'll try." Nancy couldn't believe that her voice sounded so breathy.

"Nancy, don't be nervous, you'll do great." He reached out and squeezed her hand. Then he was gone.

She stared at the closed door, amazed at her feelings. "Nancy Drew," she scolded her reflection in the mirror. "What's the matter with you?

There's only one guy in the world for you, and it's not Michael Jared."

A few minutes later she walked into the studio. The students were already at their easels, and a chair covered with drapery stood on a little platform in the center of the room.

At the sight of Nancy, Michael's blue eyes widened. Nancy self-consciously smoothed the top flounce of her skirt.

"This is Nancy Drew," Michael told the class as he led Nancy to the modeling stand. "She's filling in for Kelly today."

Nancy followed Michael onto the platform. As he was arranging the drapery on the empty chair, she spotted Rina. Nancy smiled at her, but Rina pretended not to notice.

Michael told her to pose with one leg up on the chair and an elbow resting on her knee. Michael adjusted the angle of her head. This time Nancy couldn't pretend she didn't feel a thrill as he touched her. One of the students set a timer and the pose began.

After a few minutes Nancy realized that remaining still was harder work than she'd expected. As she was glancing at the students out of the corner of her eye, she took in Rina. The redheaded girl's mouth was pursed tightly as she glanced from Nancy back to her canvas and back at Nancy again. Nancy was pleased that Rina's apparent hostility seemed to have vanished. Nancy recognized the expression of pure concentration on Rina's face. It was the same sort of concentration Nancy felt when she was deep into a case.

Meanwhile, Michael was circling the room, stopping at each student's easel. He stood a moment behind Rina and frowned at her canvas. "No," he said, just loud enough for Nancy to hear. "The color's off. Try this." He picked up a brush and mixed some colors together on her palette. He was about to touch the brush to her canvas, when Rina turned on him. "Don't you *dare* touch my work."

Michael immediately backed off. Rina's temper was beginning to impress Nancy.

The timer rang, and Michael told Nancy to take a five-minute break. Just then a tall thin girl with short, spiky bleached blond hair walked in. She carried a sketch pad and wore denim overalls and an Emerson College T-shirt. Nancy's first impression was that she seemed very young for college. Her second, even stronger, impression was that she had seen this girl before. But where?

With an adoring expression the girl followed Michael behind a glass partition in the corner of the room. Nancy watched as she handed him some papers. He signed one, then she signed another and came out. Michael then helped her set up an easel, and Nancy resumed her pose, wondering who the latecomer was.

After another half hour the students began packing up their supplies. Watching the latecomer, Nancy hazarded a smile. The girl's eyes widened, but she didn't smile back. She quickly packed her things and raced out of the room.

"Great job, Nancy," Michael said, offering her a hand to help her off the platform. He held her hand a second longer than necessary, Nancy thought. There was a tense silence. Nancy was the first to break it. "Hard work."

"I know." He sat down on the platform and stared at the floor. "I worked really hard on that painting, Nancy. *First Kiss.*"

Nancy wondered who the man behind that beautiful painting really was. She sat down next to him. He obviously needed to talk about his painting and she needed to find out more about it.

"Tell me about the painting—knowing more about it might help me find it," she said.

"What do you need to know?"

"Was it a painting of people you knew or models or what? Might one of them have had a motive to steal it?"

"Ah," Michael said. "You're good at this." He studied his hands. When he looked up his eyes were sad. "The girl isn't a model—she was someone I was very close to once. I tried capturing her many times on canvas, but *First Kiss* was the only time I succeeded. Now it's gone."

Nancy impulsively reached out and touched his arm. Their eyes met. His eyes were filled with such sorrow Nancy thought her heart would break. Michael touched her face as if he wanted to kiss her. Instead, he pulled her into a close hug.

"Nancy, please find it," he murmured.

The studio door creaked. Nancy slid out of Michael's arms and peeked past his shoulder.

She jumped up. "Ned! What are you doing here?"

Chapter

Six

"WHY AM I HERE?" Ned gasped. "I was looking for you. Sorry if I've interrupted something."

"It's not what you think—" Nancy cried.

"We were just talking," Michael started to explain. "About the case. I'm sorry. I didn't mean to cause any trouble here. . . ." He rose and quickly disappeared into his office space behind the glass partition.

"I'm sorry, Ned. I know how that looked—my hugging Michael. But it really isn't what it seemed." No matter what Ned might think, that hug had been innocent, consoling.

"I'm not that dumb," Ned said, folding his arms. "Every girl on campus has a crush on that guy. But I didn't think you'd fall for his sensitive-artist act." He punched a fist against the doorframe. "I thought I meant more to you than that."

Nancy glanced back at Michael, who was riffling through papers on his drawing table. "Ned Nickerson, you walked in here and saw me hugging Michael. Don't you hug your friends— like George or Bess? Michael's just a friend—"

"Since when?" Ned charged.

Nancy grit her teeth. "Since I took on this case and got to know him."

Ned arched his eyebrows. "I thought *everyone* was a suspect until you found the guilty party."

"Give me a break, Nickerson. Michael Jared wouldn't steal his own painting. He's got no motive."

"I could think of a few. . . ." Ned glared at Nancy. "Insurance fraud for starters. But motives are your department. Maybe when you stop making out with Michael long enough to get back to your case, you'll be able to think of a few, too."

"That's unfair!" Nancy cried, her face red with anger. "I only hugged him, Ned. But if you don't trust me, maybe we should forget it."

"Suits me fine," Ned growled, and stomped out of the room, slamming the door behind him.

"Okay!" Nancy shouted at the closed door. Then the reality of what had just happened hit her. Ned Nickerson had just walked out of her life.

Nancy's throat tightened and she felt as if she

were about to burst into tears. "Nancy?" Nancy hadn't heard Michael come up behind her.

Before she turned around to face him, she wiped away the tears that had started down her cheeks. Nancy didn't cry much, but when she did, she cried in private.

"You okay?"

"Sure." Nancy managed a weak grin. "I'm fine." The glass partition probably cut out some of the sound from the studio, but still Nancy wondered exactly how much Michael had overheard. She started to blush.

"I didn't mean to cause trouble between you two."

Nancy took a couple of deep breaths. "Don't worry, Michael, Ned and I will work this out," she said, half trying to convince herself. She looked down at her costume. "I'd better change. There are some leads I want to follow up before tonight."

After Michael came out of his office with the dressing room keys, Nancy remembered something. "By the way, who's the tall blond girl who came into class late?" she asked.

"Kate Robertson," he answered. "Today was her first class. Why?"

"I thought I recognized her, that's all." Nancy went to change her clothes, wondering why the girl was so familiar. She couldn't remember ever meeting a Kate at Emerson. Debbie's roommate was named Kate, but she wasn't due back from

Paris until next week. After Nancy locked the dressing room, she went back in the art studio to give Michael the key.

For a moment Nancy stood in the door just observing him. Maybe Ned was right—maybe even Michael should be considered a suspect in the robbery. Insurance was a plausible motive, but Nancy couldn't imagine him needing money. He was a household name at the age of twenty-six. No, Ned was dead wrong this time. Besides, Michael was proud of that painting. He wanted it to be seen.

She handed him the key. "I've got to go now. But I promise I'm going to find your painting."

Michael's blue eyes glowed and he took her hand. "I know that Nancy. If anyone can find *First Kiss*, it's you."

Nancy left the art building and pondered her next move. Doubling back to the student union, she found a phone and called the galleries George had listed for her. So far no one had attempted to sell a painting resembling the *First Kiss* anywhere nearby. Next, she dialed the last sporting goods store on her list to ask if the store had recently sold any climbing ropes.

"As if I've got nothing better to do than check inventory for anyone who just happens to call," the clerk grumbled into the receiver. "Why do you need to know?"

Nancy forced herself to sound polite. "A friend's in trouble." She dropped her voice to a whisper. "I promised I wouldn't tell *anyone* about it, but knowing who bought ropes from you might help solve this guy's problems."

To her amazement it worked. "If you put it that way," the clerk relented. "I'll check my inventory." He put Nancy on hold. A twangy country-western tune blared in her ear. "We sold a rope this morning," the clerk announced, returning to the line several minutes later, "but that's the only one in the last month."

"A credit purchase or cash?" Nancy asked, curious even though it had been bought after the break-in.

"It was a cash purchase."

"Can you describe the buyer?" Nancy asked.

"I wasn't working this morning—Randy was. But he's off now. He'll be here tomorrow morning, if you want to check with him then."

Nancy felt exasperated. Every lead seemed to put her on hold. The campus clock's gonging made her realize she had to get back to the Theta Pi house soon to meet George. As she threaded her way across campus toward Greek Row, she reasoned that the rope that had been purchased earlier that day could be connected to the theft if the thief had needed to replace the stolen rope.

As she approached the Theta Pi house, she saw Brook, Chris, and Rosie seated under the massive oak tree in the front yard.

"What's going on?" Nancy asked, joining the group. Brook pointed at the roof and Nancy saw the sorority house cat crouched above one of the eaves, looking terrified.

"How'd Kabuki get up there?" Nancy asked.

Chris shrugged. "The real question is, how will she get down?"

"Rina, that's how," said Rosie, motioning toward the big tree. Nancy peered up through the branches. Rina's red braid bobbed as she shimmied up the tree and out along a thick limb that hung out over the roof. "It's okay, Buki," Rina called softly to the cat.

Rina finally reached the roof. Stretching out, she grabbed the cat and pulled her in close to her chest. Rina backed off the thick branch, then climbed down the trunk. Reaching the ground, she kissed the cat's nose, then passed Kabuki to Brook.

"She's scared." Rina picked up her knapsack and portfolio off the grass. Tossing her braid over her shoulder, she headed for her car.

"Thanks, Rina," Brook called.

Rina waved her hand but didn't look back.

Nancy had watched the scene, fascinated. She hadn't considered Rina a suspect in the museum robbery. But why not? Rina needed money, she obviously was very agile, and if she was Bryan's old girlfriend, she probably knew all about climbing ropes—and the timing of his rounds at the museum. She had to be a suspect. Then Nancy remembered—Rosie said that she and Rina had been ushering the night before. But was ushering a foolproof alibi? Nancy needed to find out.

"Rina looked good up there," Nancy said to Brook as the girls headed inside the house. "Is she into climbing like Bryan?"

"Not that I know of. Art is her thing."

While Brook headed to the kitchen to get Kabuki some food, Nancy scanned the call board in the back hall, hoping there would be a message from Ned. A lump lodged in her throat as she ran her eyes down the board a second time. There were several folded message slips for Debbie, but nothing for her.

In the living room Nancy curled up on a couch, a hollow feeling in her chest. Maybe this time their fight was too serious to be made up.

Her eyes strayed to an overstuffed chair across the room. It was heaped with glittery antique flapper dresses. Nancy had forgotten about that night's Omega Chi dance.

Chris collapsed on the couch next to Nancy. "Aren't those dresses great?" she said. "My grandmother sent me a box of them. They belonged to her mother, my great-grandmother. She was a singer in a jazz club in Harlem in the twenties, and she had all these costumes stored in the attic. I know you've already got a dress," she said to Nancy, "but if anybody else needs a dress for tonight, I've got a bunch."

"They're fantastic," Brook said, walking into the room. She held a silver-beaded chemise up to her shoulders and studied her reflection in the mirror above the fireplace.

"Looks great," Nancy commented, wondering if she'd be needing her dress for that night's Omega Chi party after all.

Debbie came in the front door and walked right by them. "Deb," Rosie called after her. "Bryan just called on the house phone. He said he got no answer on your phone and your answering machine was turned off. He wanted you to call right away."

"Okay," Debbie answered.

"Mrs. Shephard called, too. Twice," Brook added. "She says it's really important."

"Got it," Debbie called back.

"Hey, I hear you modeled for Jared's class today," Rosie said, eyeing Nancy.

"Are you kidding?" Brook gasped. "Tell all. You're an honorary sister for the weekend, and we should be the first to know what Michael 'The Hunk' Jared is really like."

Nancy felt a blush creep up her neck. "He's very nice and he's miserable about the theft of his painting."

"Hmmm," Rosie said, her dark eyes sparkling. "Why do I get the feeling you're not telling us everything you know about this guy?"

Talking about the painting class reminded Nancy to ask the girls if they knew anyone named Kate Robertson.

"Of course," Chris said, stroking Kabuki. "Kate is a Theta Pi. She's Debbie's roommate."

So that's why the blond girl looked so familiar, thought Nancy. She'd never met Kate, but she must have seen a photograph of her. "When did Kate get back from Paris?"

"She's not back," Rosie said.

"But Kate Robertson was in art class this afternoon," Nancy told the girls.

"I don't think so," Brook said. "We'd have seen her. But ask Debbie. She'd know."

When Nancy got to Debbie's room, the door was closed. Nancy couldn't tell if Debbie was talking to someone inside the room, or someone on the phone. All she heard was Debbie speaking hysterically.

"I don't care how hard it is to do. You've got to put it back."

Nancy's heart stopped. Put what back?

First Kiss? she wondered.

And who was Debbie talking to? Her mysterious roommate Kate Robertson suddenly back from Paris—*if* she'd ever been in Paris at all? Or someone else? Nancy's throat went dry. When Debbie came home a few minutes ago, Rosie had told her to call someone right away. Nancy just remembered who.

Bryan.

Chapter

Seven

WITHOUT WARNING, Debbie's door swung open.

"I was just about to knock," Nancy blurted out as Debbie, who was dressed in a robe, practically bumped into her.

"Oh, it's you." Debbie closed the door behind her. "More questions?" Debbie snapped. Then bit her lip. "Sorry, I didn't mean to yell at you. I'm just exhausted. Any leads on Michael's painting?"

"No." Nancy had to find out who Debbie had been talking to. "How's Bryan?" Nancy asked.

"Why?" Debbie sounded defensive.

"I thought I heard you talking to him on the telephone just now." Nancy said.

"I haven't spoken to him all day," she said curtly, starting for the staircase.

Then who had been on the phone—or in the room? Nancy followed Debbie up the stairs to the bathroom. "When did Kate come back?"

"Kate?" She looked at Nancy as if she'd sprouted a second head. "I told you she's in Paris."

"No way. I saw Kate in art class today. Rina was there, too."

Debbie gripped the banister and shook her head firmly. "Nancy, whoever you saw, it wasn't Kate."

"Michael told me the student's name," Nancy insisted. "Kate Robertson."

"Then Michael's wrong." Debbie had reached the second-floor landing. "Or else there's another Kate Robertson at Emerson."

Intrigued, Nancy trailed Debbie into the large bathroom. Debbie grabbed a blue plastic box from one of the lockers. Nancy followed her to a shower stall. Debbie turned on the water and tested it with her hand. "Are you expecting to find Kate in the shower or something?"

Nancy ignored her sarcasm. "The girl in Michael's art class was a tall, gangling girl with short bleached-blond hair," Nancy said. "Is that your Kate Robertson?"

Debbie blew out her breath impatiently. "No. 'My' Kate is big—a little heavy—and her hair's brown."

So it was a different Kate, Nancy decided. Then she asked, "At lunchtime you were talking to a girl with long brown hair, in a red shirt."

The barest hint of surprise or panic—Nancy wasn't sure which—flickered across Debbie's face. Nancy sensed she was honing in on Debbie's secret. "It was in the quad," she said, trying to provoke some reaction in Debbie.

Debbie's face stayed calm, but her knuckles whitened as she gripped her hands into fists. "I don't know who you're talking about. I talked to lots of people today." She turned her back on Nancy and untied her robe.

Nancy didn't budge. "Who were you talking to just now? In your room?"

Debbie kept her back turned but gave a careless shrug. "Nancy, I don't know what you think you overheard. It was probably a TV."

"Sure." For the moment Nancy had to concede defeat. Getting a hold on Debbie was like trying to get a grip on a wet fish. She kept slithering out of reach.

Debbie poked her head out of the shower. "Maybe if you stopped wasting your time hounding me with dumb questions about Kate Robertson, you might actually solve this crime." Debbie yanked the curtain shut.

Nancy slammed the bathroom door behind her. "Aaargh!" she groaned in frustration. Nancy prided herself on her talent to psych people out. But so far she'd scored a big fat zero with Debbie.

On her way back downstairs, she picked up a campus directory and flipped through it. She was more confused than ever. The only Kate Robertson listed was right here at Theta Pi.

Then Nancy remembered something. Debbie's roommate was an impressive copyist. Could her skills have something to do with the stolen painting? Nancy headed straight back down to Debbie's room.

Nancy knocked on her door. No one answered. She tried to turn the doorknob. Locked. Why would Debbie lock her door just to take a shower? Unless there was someone inside— someone who had slipped out while Nancy was upstairs questioning Debbie. Nancy raced into the kitchen.

"Has anyone passed through here in the last couple of minutes?" Nancy asked Trish Hardcastle, who was at the microwave nuking some popcorn.

"Nope," the blond girl replied.

Hearing laughter outside, Nancy peeked out the back screen door. Mindy and Rosie had turned lawn hoses on each other, and both were drenched. No one else was around.

If Kate had been in Debbie's room, she was gone. In the living room Brook and Chris were on the couch, petting Kabuki. "Do either of you have a picture of Debbie's roommate, Kate?" Nancy asked.

The girls acted surprised. "Yeah, sure. I can find one," Chris replied. She went to the bookcase under the windows and pulled out a photo album. Chris flipped through the pages. "Here."

She pointed out pictures of Kate, a tall big-boned girl with prominent cheekbones. The blond girl in Michael's class was also tall but she was very thin. There was no resemblance between the two.

"Where is everyone?" George yelled from the front door. She poked her head in the living room and grinned. She was wearing purple jogging shorts and a blue tank top. Her brown curls were damp from the heat. "Hi, Nancy," she said. "I'm beat. I'd better take a nap before the party. But come on up and I'll tell you some good news."

Nancy followed George to the room she was sharing for the weekend with Mindy. George flopped facedown on Kirstin's pink-flowered bedspread.

"How was the climbing gym?" Nancy dropped into the rocking chair and propped her feet on the windowsill. She scrutinized George. "And why are you so sleepy? You're never tired."

George smiled, her eyes still shut. "The gym was great. It's huge, with all these climbing routes. It was a tough workout, so we went in a hot tub later. I feel like Jell-O. Beyond relaxed."

"You said you had good news."

George opened her eyes. "I do. Bryan's not your thief. We didn't need his rope for the gym," George continued, "because the gym provides ropes. Bryan's new rope is in his Jeep."

"How new?"

"Brand-new. Bryan said he bought it for his trip next weekend to Indian Rock."

"Do climbers usually have more than one rope?"

George groaned. "Yes, Nan, good climbers do. There are different strengths for different types of climbs. But ropes aren't cheap. I doubt a student like Bryan would have a bunch of ropes. He's not your bad guy here."

Nancy decided to keep her suspicions about Bryan to herself for the moment. "But I am a little worried"—she paused—"about *you.* Aren't Bryan and Debbie still an item?"

George fingered one of her curls. "I don't think so. He's called her a couple of times today to have it out with her. He's miffed she stood him up at lunch, and he said things haven't been great between them—even before the robbery." George hesitated before continuing. "Don't worry, I'm going to the dance with you and Ned, not Bryan. He's got to sort things out with Debbie first, though I think they're about to break up."

"Debbie told us that, too." Nancy got up. "But I'm not sure I trust anything that Debbie says these days."

George sat up and suddenly seemed wide-awake. "You dug up something on Debbie?"

Before Nancy could respond, Rosie Lopez's voice came on the house intercom, giggling. "Nancy Drew, someone's here to see you."

"Sounds like a male someone." George laughed. "Why doesn't she just say Ned?"

71

"Because it's probably not Ned," Nancy said ruefully, and stood up. "We had a real fight."

"He didn't seem that upset at lunch—"

"It got worse later," Nancy said, her heart in her throat. "I'm not sure I'm going to the dance at all." George's mouth fell open. "I can't explain now. Maybe it's Sergeant Weinberg about the case," Nancy said. But as she left the room, someone else came to mind. Michael. Maybe Michael had come to see her.

"Nancy?"

"Ned?" Nancy practically shouted for joy. She bounced down the last few steps and stopped a few feet away from Ned. He was dressed in running shorts and had one hand behind his back. He looked embarrassed and a little surprised.

"Were you expecting someone else?"

Nancy blushed. "No, I mean—I thought it was Sergeant Weinberg. About the case . . ."

"I'm sorry," they both said in unison, then burst out laughing. Ned handed Nancy a white rose. "Peace?"

"Peace." Nancy accepted the rose and smiled up at Ned.

"Is there someplace we can talk?" he asked.

Peering up into his eyes, all she wanted to do was kiss him, but she needed to clear the air between them first. "Outside." Nancy led Ned behind the sorority house and down a path that led to the lake. Ned was the first to speak.

"I was way out of line this afternoon, about Jared. You were right, Nan. I hug female friends all the time. It's natural. It has nothing to do with my feelings for you."

Nancy felt as if a truckload of bricks had been lifted off her shoulders. "I'm glad you understand," she said quietly. "But I was wrong, too, Ned." She paused and stared up into his eyes. "I should have understood where you were coming from—and—" She took a deep breath and forced herself to be honest. "You weren't completely wrong."

She felt Ned tense up. "But mostly wrong," she added quickly, touching his arm. They continued walking and stopped just short of the boathouse. Nancy pushed her hair off her face and gazed directly up at Ned. "Michael is attractive, and for a second there—" Nancy swallowed hard. "But even when I was hugging him I knew it was you I wanted, Ned. Not Michael Jared."

Ned searched her eyes and a slow smile spread across his face. "You know what I love most about you, Nancy Drew?"

She shook her head slowly.

Ned put his hands on her face and tilted her chin up. "You don't know how to lie. You always tell the truth." Then he bent down and Nancy tightly wrapped her arms around him as they shared a kiss. After pulling apart, they strolled down to the end of the boat dock, and Nancy nestled her head in the crook of Ned's arm. She felt as if she had finally come home. "Tell me about your case," Ned said.

When Nancy told Ned about the girl in art class, his eyes flashed. "I bet some student who's nuts about Jared decided to pose as Kate just to get into his class."

"Maybe." That was definitely a possibility.

"And your suspicions about Bryan, Nancy. You're way off track there."

Nancy didn't answer. She wondered herself why she was so unwilling to cross Bryan off her list. She glanced at her watch. "We'd better get back."

When Nancy and Ned finally approached the Theta Pi house, they heard laughter spilling out onto the porch. "I'll pick you up at nine, Nan," Ned said. After kissing her on the cheek, he jogged back down the steps.

Inside, the girls were modeling their costumes for one another. Certain she'd be spending the evening with Ned, Nancy was eager to join in the fun. Mindy, Chris, and Rosie were all almost dressed. Trish and Debbie sat curled up on a couch, both still in their robes. Beside Debbie was an opaque white garment bag.

Debbie barely returned Nancy's smile, and Nancy couldn't blame her. She'd put Debbie through some pretty heavy questioning earlier. Nancy walked over to the coffee table and fished through Chris's box of accessories.

"Try these beads," Chris suggested, handing Nancy a long strand of artificial pearls.

"And *this* is definitely you," Rosie said, plopping a beaded green cap on Chris's dark hair. Chris's green tunic skimmed her figure, showing off her curves.

"Try on your dress, Debbie," Mindy urged as she slipped into a pair of black heels. "I saw it when Trish brought it from the shop, but I'm dying to see it on you."

Debbie fingered the zipper on her garment bag and made a face. "Why bother? I'm not even sure I'm going to the party." She blew her bangs out of her face. "I haven't spoken to Bryan yet." She stared at Nancy defiantly.

"Come on, Deb."

"Mindy swears you'll win the costume contest."

Debbie began to smile. "Even if I end up going stag?"

"Stag?" Nancy repeated.

"As I told you last night, Bryan and I aren't getting on real well, and I'm not in the mood to spend a whole evening with him."

For a moment the living room grew quiet, then Chris giggled. "You won't stay solo long at the dance." She gave Debbie a friendly poke in the ribs. "Half of us are going stag anyway. It's getting late. Put it on."

Chris plunked herself down next to Debbie and unzipped the bag on her lap. Nancy gasped with the other girls as the lamplight glinted off the jade green sequins. Debbie colored with pleasure and started to slip the dress off its hanger.

"Ohhhh!" she screamed, and dropped the dress and hanger as if they were on fire.

"Your dress!" Chris cried, jumping off the couch. The open garment bag slid off her lap and green sequins scattered over the carpet.

Nancy picked up Debbie's beautiful flapper costume. The dress dangled from the pink padded hanger like a bunch of glittery ribbons. Someone had taken a knife and slashed the dress to shreds.

Chapter
Eight

"WHY?" DEBBIE WAILED, collapsing in a heap on the couch. "Why would anyone do this?"

"Who hates you this much?" Nancy asked.

Footsteps clattered down the stairs. "Hey, what's going on down here?" George asked as she burst into the room. She was in her silver sheath. Trish was right behind her, an eye pencil in her hand. Only one of her large green eyes was made up.

At the sight of the dress, George gasped.

"I don't believe this." Trish took the dress from Nancy. "This time Rina's gone too far."

"Hold it, Trish," Brook warned. "You have no proof."

"Who else hates Debbie?" Trish tossed the dress aside. "And who was here when I brought the dresses in? Rina." She gave the belt of her blue-and-white robe a jerk.

George's eyebrows shot up. Nancy cautioned her with a glance. "Calm down, Trish," Nancy said quietly. "Tell me exactly what happened with the dress."

"Debbie and I bought our dresses last week at a vintage shop off Main Street," Trish said. "They needed to be altered. I picked them up this morning. When I brought them back, a couple of girls were here—"

"Who?" Nancy asked quickly.

Trish thought a minute. "Juanita and Mindy. I showed them the dresses. Rina walked in just then. She said she really liked Debbie's dress and saw me leave it in the front closet."

"And when did you take the dress to your room?" Nancy asked Debbie.

"During a break this afternoon," Debbie told her. "Trish left a note on my door saying the dress was in the closet."

"So anyone in this house could have read that note," Nancy pointed out.

"Yes," Trish admitted reluctantly, "but only Rina would want to hurt Debbie."

Chris blew out her breath and frowned. "I can't imagine Rina doing this."

"Me, either," Debbie said, her voice quavering. "Besides, I know she didn't." Nancy barely caught Debbie's last words.

"How do you know?" Nancy asked quickly.

"I just do." Debbie blew her nose.

"You know who did this, don't you?" Nancy's question stunned the room.

"Of course not," Debbie snapped.

Trish gazed at Nancy as if she were crazy. Nancy shrugged, but she was convinced Debbie was shielding someone. Rina? But why?

Debbie began to sob. Brook put an arm around her to comfort her.

"It'll be okay, Debbie," Chris said. She picked up the box of her grandmother's dresses. "You're coming to that party tonight—no way you're staying here alone. You can wear one of Granny Lula's costumes." Debbie raised her head.

"Hey," Rosie declared, "sorority sisters help each other out."

"Thanks, guys," Debbie murmured.

Nancy was frustrated by Debbie's silence, but she was worried, too. "I don't mean to be a party pooper, but this is a pretty violent practical joke." She glanced at the dress. "Maybe we'd better lock the doors even during the day and keep the ground-floor windows shut."

The girls acted scared as they disbanded to get ready for the party.

"Tell me about Rina," Nancy said to Brook as they headed upstairs. "She doesn't seem like the other girls in this sorority. I'm surprised she got pledged."

"She was a legacy, which means a relative was a Theta Pi. We had to take her," Brook explained. "And I understand Rina's aunt told her she'd pay her housing if she pledged—kind of a bribe. People do things for their own reasons."

Nancy nodded. Her work as a detective had proved that time and again.

"After she pledged," Brook continued, "Rina went her own way. She got along okay here—until Bryan and Debbie started dating. Then Rina acted as if we were *all* against her. I guess she's angry at the world."

"Angry enough to slash a dress?"

Brook shrugged. "I don't know." She glanced at the clock on the landing. "We'd better get moving," she said, heading for her room.

Nancy showered and changed and was ready to greet Ned when he showed up at the front door. Twirling, she showed off her short, black fringed dress, curls of her reddish blond hair peeking out from under a black cloche hat. "Like it?" Nancy asked.

Ned poked his straw boater hat to the back of his head and whistled. "I love it."

Nancy thought that Ned looked great, too. He was dressed in a white double-breasted suit, striped shirt, and red bow tie.

When they reached the Omega Chi house, the party was in full swing. George had come earlier with Mindy and Rosie to help set up. She waved Ned and Nancy over to the buffet table, where she was serving punch.

"Great party!" she shouted over the music.

One of Ned's frat brothers, Howie Little,

strode up and pounded Ned on the back. He grinned at Nancy. "Hear you turned up just in time to play detective again."

Ned groaned as George handed him a cup of punch. "Tell me about it."

Nancy sighed. "Mysteries just seem to follow me."

"Don't sound so sad about it," Howie said. "Half the girls in this room would love to be in your shoes—lending a helping hand to our artist heartthrob."

Nancy felt Ned tense up and quickly stifled the desire to kick Howie. Instead she gazed up at Ned, batted her eyes, and said with sugary sweetness, "Oh, I thought you were going to say they'd love to be in my shoes because I'm here with Ned."

Howie threw back his head and laughed. "Since this is such a dependent relationship, I guess I'll have to ask if I can borrow him a second. We're having trouble with the sound system." With that Howie steered Ned away.

Nancy glanced around. Strobe lights had been hooked up to the ceiling fixtures. The flickering lights and dancing bodies made it hard to identify people. She did see Chris, which made her wonder which of Chris's dresses Debbie had chosen to wear.

Nancy spotted Bryan first. He was the only guy in the room not dressed in twenties-style clothing. He was wearing blue jeans and an EC T-shirt. Yellow and red lights flickered across his face and glinted off his earring. Debbie was half hidden in the shadows. A feather jutted up from her white headband, and she looked cool and elegant in a white feathery chemise. Nancy could see Debbie did not feel cool. Her cheeks were flushed, and her gestures were agitated.

Nancy wove her way through the press of dancers until she could hear Bryan and Debbie. Nancy stood close to the couple, pretending to study a poster on the wall.

"It's over, Bryan. . . ." Debbie's voice shook.

"Why don't you come out and say it—it's my fault you lost your job."

"No," Debbie insisted. "It's just not working between us—you'd rather be rock climbing."

Bryan threw his hands up. "You're jealous—"

"Jealous?" Debbie sounded flabbergasted.

"Of George. We went to the Climbing Wall."

"George? Nancy's friend?" Debbie paused.

Nancy winced. Then Debbie surprised her. "She's nice, Bryan. More your type. I don't mean to hurt you, but we just don't have that much in common."

Nancy had heard enough. The conversation had nothing to do with her case. She turned to leave.

"It's since the robbery that we suddenly don't have anything in common—" Bryan said. Nancy froze in her tracks.

"Let's not get into that again. I've heard enough about the theft of Michael's painting from Nancy. She's been following me as if I'm a suspect—and I know she suspects you, too," Debbie warned.

Bryan narrowed his eyes. "Why do you say that?"

"Questions she's been asking. Anyway, I don't want to talk about the robbery now."

With that Debbie turned and walked off toward the kitchen. Nancy watched as Bryan marched right up to George and pulled her onto the dance floor. It was a slow tune, and Bryan wrapped his arms around George, pulling her close.

"Hey, I thought he was dating Debbie?" Ned's voice made Nancy turn around.

"Not anymore."

"That was sudden."

"Wasn't it?" Nancy said, wondering what kind of person Bryan was. First, he dated Rina, then switched to Debbie. Then minutes after Debbie dumped him, he was coming on strong to George. Did he really like George? Or did he think by making friends with George he'd have an inside track into Nancy's investigation.

Ned didn't give her much time to think about it. The music had changed and the band was playing a Charleston. "Let's cut some rug," Ned said, using twenties slang badly.

Nancy blew out her breath. Part of her wanted to see where Debbie had gone. Another part wanted to hang out with George and Bryan to figure what Bryan was up to. Instead she opted to dance with Ned. "You're on, Nickerson," she said, pulling him onto the dance floor. Nancy let herself forget all about her investigation and threw herself into a wild Charleston.

Ned matched his energy to hers and soon they were the only couple on the dance floor. The whole room was clapping and cheering them on. When the music ended, the crowd roared. Nancy sagged into Ned's arms and grinned.

"We're some team!" he shouted into her ear.

Nancy was smiling so hard she thought her face might break. George, Chris, and Brook forced their way up to Nancy and thumped her on the back. "Great dancing, Nan," George crowed. Nancy looked past George's shoulder, expecting Bryan.

"Where's Bryan?"

"Phone call" was all Nancy heard. Did that mean he had made or received one? Nancy headed for the foyer.

Bryan was on the hall phone, his back to the room. Nancy joined the line outside the ladies' room. "All right!" he shouted enthusiastically into the receiver. He pumped one fist into the air. "Monday night. My future is made."

Monday—that was when Bryan was having dinner with art collector Ian Sanders. Was he planning to sell *First Kiss* to Sanders? Nancy hoped to hear more, but Bryan hung up and joined a group of guys on the porch.

Hours later the band played its last song. The lights were turned out, but Nancy and Ned still swayed in the circle of each other's arms. "I hate to spoil a good thing," Ned murmured, "but in case Ms. Sherlock Holmes hasn't noticed, the music has stopped."

"The band, Ned, not the music," Nancy whispered into the white linen of Ned's jacket.

"And to think," Ned said huskily, "only this afternoon I thought I'd lost you to another guy."

Nancy leaned back and looked up at Ned. She couldn't read his expression in the dark, but from the way he was holding her, she knew he was no longer worried.

That night Nancy couldn't sleep, so she grabbed her notebook and tiptoed downstairs. She settled herself on a couch in the den and settled in to review her notes on the case. She didn't remember falling asleep, but she woke to a sound outside.

Nancy rose and stretched her cramped limbs. Sunlight poured in through the windows. The day was already warm.

Gravel crunched in the driveway as Nancy made her way to the window. A white Subaru was backing out to the street with Debbie in the driver's seat. Next to her was a girl with spiky bleached hair.

It was the girl from Michael's art class.

Chapter

Nine

NANCY RACED OUTSIDE, but Debbie's car was gone. So Debbie did know the blond girl.

Back inside, Nancy found Juanita at the kitchen table giggling over a comic strip. "Did you see Debbie leave?"

"Uh-huh." Juanita stretched and yawned.

"Who was with her?" Nancy asked.

"Nobody." Juanita sipped her coffee.

"Are you sure?" The kitchen windows looked out on the yard and the parking lot.

"Sure I'm sure. Debbie headed out alone. Oh, breakfast's not until nine on the weekend." She put her cup in the dishwasher and left.

Nancy was puzzled. How did Debbie sneak the girl past Juanita? Maybe Debbie's room would provide some clues. Nancy knocked on Debbie's door. No one answered and the door was locked—again. Nancy felt in her bathrobe pocket for a metal nail file. With the file she forced the lock open. Nancy went in and locked the door from inside.

She knew she had to work fast. The room seemed to be exactly the same. If the blond girl was crashing here, she was traveling light. No suitcase, duffel, or knapsack in sight. One desk was cluttered with notebooks, textbooks, and files. A mug with DEBBIE printed on the side was near the PC. The mug was full of pencils.

Nancy opened a manila envelope next to the PC. Inside was a computer printout of classes for Debbie Lakin and forms for fall registration.

Kate's registration packet, Nancy remembered. Nancy turned quickly to check the other desk, and her elbow knocked over the mug of pencils. "Shoot!" Nancy exclaimed.

Just then footsteps sounded in the hall.

"I thought you said Debbie left?" Rosie's voice floated through the closed door.

"She did," Juanita said.

"Someone's in there!" Rosie sounded terrified. "Nancy said to be careful."

Someone tried the door. "It's locked." Rosie sounded relieved. "Probably just a mouse. Better get Buki back on mouse duty." Nancy remained perfectly still until the laughter faded down the hall. Close call, Nancy thought, and straightened up the mug and put the pencils back.

Time was running out. Kate's desk was neat.

The calendar was still turned to June. Nancy tried the drawers. "Yes," Nancy cheered softly. Kate Robertson's registration packet was inside. Nancy riffled through it. She stopped when a familiar name caught her eye. Listed on a schedule of classes was Painting 204; Instructor, M. Jared. So Kate Robertson was registered, and someone else had showed up in her place.

Nothing more of interest turned up in the desk. Nancy scanned the room once more, convinced she must be missing something. She caught a glimpse of something white stuck between a footlocker and bed. She took a closer look. It was a small painter's canvas. She picked it up carefully. Her pulse quickened as she recognized herself in the gypsy costume she'd modeled for Michael's class. She touched a corner of the canvas with her pinky. The paint was still wet. The painting obviously belonged to the blond, the girl Michael said was Kate Robertson.

Nancy put the painting back and opened the footlocker. Inside was a small packet of art supplies. The shrink-wrap had been torn open, but someone had obviously tried to seal it again.

Then she turned her attention to a large newsprint drawing pad. She opened it. On the first page was a detailed sketch of *First Kiss*. When had Kate had a chance to see the painting?

Nancy was stumped.

She tore the sketch of *First Kiss* out of the pad. She might need evidence when she confronted

Debbie. The sound of voices in the hall startled Nancy. She couldn't risk being discovered.

Poking her head out Debbie's open window, she saw the coast was clear and climbed out. "Ugh!" she grunted as her bare feet sank into the wet loam of the flower bed. She frowned. It hadn't rained in days. Then she remembered Rosie and Mindy having a water fight the day before with the garden hose. Using the shrubbery for cover, Nancy edged her way toward the back door. Glancing down at the ground, she saw a line of footprints. Someone wearing sneakers with a foot about the same size as Nancy's had sneaked through the bushes earlier. The trail led from under Debbie's window toward the parking lot. No wonder Juanita hadn't seen the blond girl—she must have gone out Debbie's window.

Nancy had made a date with Ned to go to the Climbing Wall. The new gym was sponsoring a competition, and Bryan was one of the contestants. After Nancy picked Ned up in her blue Mustang, she told him what she had learned.

"So Debbie is hiding this girl and allowing her to assume her roommate's identity," Ned said thoughtfully. "This new girl must have sketched the stolen painting. But why?"

"Don't know yet." She glanced at Ned and grinned. "Maybe you'd like to shut your window, Ned. Your hair looks like Debbie's friend's—it's sticking up in all directions."

Ned ran a hand through his hair. "What else did you find out this morning?"

Nancy made a sharp left turn. "I talked to the guy at Marshalls who sold a rope yesterday."

"What did he say?" Ned asked.

"Since the buyer paid cash, the clerk didn't have his name, but he said the guy was tall, muscular, with long sun-streaked brown hair, and he seemed to be an experienced climber. He bought a rope, a harness—the works. Oh, and a green headband and a purple windbreaker."

"Colorful," Ned joked. "But, Nan, long brown hair, tall, climbing experience describe a lot of guys."

"Or it could be Bryan." Nancy glanced at Ned. He was frowning. "Hey, I know!" he exclaimed. "Bryan always wears a gold earring. Did the customer have an earring?"

"I asked," Nancy replied. "He couldn't remember an earring."

"There it is." Ned pointed to a green warehouse on their right with the Climbing Wall painted above the door. Nancy parked her car at the edge of the crowded lot.

"I also talked to Rosie Lopez this morning about that play she and Rina ushered for on Thursday night," Nancy said, turning off the ignition. "The last act started at ten o'clock and lasted about an hour. Rosie saw Rina afterward, but not during the performance."

"So you're thinking Rina could have had

enough time to slip out, rob the museum, and return to the theater."

They faced each other. "It's a possibility."

"And her motive?"

"Rina needs money for tuition," Nancy said. "She is a good climber, Ned. I saw her move along tree branches like a monkey. She's Bryan's old girlfriend, and I bet she knows all about climbing gear."

"And what does Jared think about all this?" Ned asked, staring out the windshield.

Nancy stopped a smile from forming. She detected a note of jealousy beneath Ned's casual tone. "I don't know. I haven't had a chance to ask him yet."

Ned frowned.

Nancy gave a careless shrug. "I'll fill him in tomorrow at the gallery opening. All he cares about is getting his painting back."

"Right." Ned sounded skeptical.

When Ned opened the gym door a minute later, the roar of the crowd was deafening.

George had told Nancy the space was huge, but she was still amazed at the size as she and Ned wove their way through the crowd. Along one side of the mammoth building, artificial rock walls towered up to the arched ceiling. Craning her neck, Nancy could only see the top of the wall. The lower half was hidden behind a wall of spectators.

"Look, there's George!" Nancy pointed to the

top of the crowded bleachers. George was jumping up and down, cheering a climber on.

"I bet Bryan's competing now." Ned grinned. Ned found an open space against the wall. Nancy squeezed in next to him. It was a minute before she got her first glimpse of the climber.

He was as graceful as a dancer as he moved from hold to hold. Even from that distance Nancy could feel his determination as he clipped his rope onto the bolts that dotted the rock wall.

Nancy shielded her eyes against the glare of the overhead lights as the climber's whole body came into view. She couldn't see the color of his headband, but she'd know that hair anywhere. "It *is* Bryan!" she shouted over the roar of the crowd and grabbed Ned's arm. "He's really good." Nancy turned and met Ned's shining eyes.

"Campus grapevine says he's one of the best." Ned whooped and let out a huge cheer as Bryan pulled far ahead of his nearest competitor.

Nancy leaned back on her heels to see Bryan better. As he pulled himself toward the top of the wall and out of the glare of the lights, Nancy's heart sank. Bryan's headband was brilliant green.

Chapter

Ten

"Bry-an! Bry-an! Bry-an!"

The chant started in a corner of the bleachers where George and the Omega Chis were sitting. As Bryan slapped the giant gold star painted on the top of the wall, the room roared. Only Nancy was quiet, her eyes fixed on Bryan's headband.

Bryan pushed off, dropping fast, kicking off from the rock a couple of times as he slid down. For a moment Nancy lost sight of him, then the crowd broke up in time for her to see him jump the last couple of feet to the floor. He threw his head back and pumped his fist in the air.

"Way to go, Barbour!" Ned yelled.

By now other climbers had reached the top and were rappelling down, but Bryan had won, no contest. Nancy gazed up at George. Even from a distance Nancy could see that her friend was grinning from ear to ear.

Nancy wished for once in her life she weren't a detective. She was tired of discovering facts that could hurt her dearest friends.

Ned stopped clapping and scooped Nancy up in a big hug. "I told you he's the best." After Ned met Nancy's gaze, he slowly put her down, searching her eyes the whole time. "What's wrong?"

"Ned," Nancy shouted over the roar of the crowd. "Bryan's headband. It's green!"

"So?" Ned shouted back. "Lots of people wear green headbands. It's just a coincidence. If not, Bryan will be able to explain."

"Maybe he will," she conceded, though her suspicions about Bryan were growing stronger.

When the competition was over, Bryan and a small-boned, dark-haired woman were declared the winners, each of them coming forward to receive a trophy.

"I'm glad we got here in time to see Bryan climb," Ned said excitedly as they made their way over toward Bryan.

Nancy nodded absentmindedly and waved at Bryan, who was walking away from George with a white-haired woman.

"Wasn't Bryan outrageous?" George was beaming.

"Great," Ned agreed.

"He has to do an interview for a climbing

magazine," George said, all smiles. "He said he'd catch up with us at the Waterside Inn."

Soon Nancy, Ned, and George were headed toward the small restaurant outside of town. When they sat down outside at a redwood table on the deck, Nancy recognized some other climbers at the salad bar.

"Isn't that Dr. Morrison?" George tapped Nancy's wrist. Nancy turned. The museum curator was pushing his chair back from a table nearby. A thin, tanned man dressed in chinos and deck shoes was with him. Dr. Morrison smiled at Nancy cordially but didn't stop to talk.

A minute later Nancy spotted Bryan through the white trellis that bordered the deck. "Bryan's already here," Nancy announced.

George waved, but Bryan didn't see her. He headed straight for Dr. Morrison's friend. The two talked animatedly while the curator listened.

"Who's that with Dr. Morrison?" Nancy asked.

Ned shrugged. "Never seen him before."

When Bryan finally moved out onto the deck, Nancy could see his gym bag, which was slung over one arm. It was open and the sleeve of a purple windbreaker poked out. Nancy tensed as a cheer for Bryan went up from climbers at the salad bar.

"All right, Bryan," Ned joined in.

Nancy was startled by Ned's enthusiastic greeting. Was Ned blind? Didn't he see that purple windbreaker?

A green headband might be written off as coincidence, but a green headband *and* a purple windbreaker? Nancy was certain now that Bryan was the guy who had bought the rope and other climbing supplies at Marshalls on Friday.

"That was Ian Sanders with Dr. Morrison," Bryan told them when he sat down. His cheeks were pink from excitement and his hair wet from a shower. "You remember," he told George in an excited voice, "the art collector I crewed for last year."

While they ate, Nancy wondered about the friendship between the museum curator and the collector. Did their relationship somehow connect to her case? Bryan might be able to shed some light on that. But now she had something else to ask the climber. She waited until they were having dessert.

"Bryan, why did you buy two climbing ropes in the last month, first at Outdoors Unlimited and then at Marshalls?"

Bryan's jaw dropped. "How do you know that?" Before Nancy could answer, he heaved a huge sigh. "Who am I kidding? It's your job to figure things out. I thought I was being framed. I needed new gear to show if anyone asked. Besides, I needed equipment for the contest today and for Indian Rock."

"Framed?" George repeated, stunned.

"The night of the robbery, when I saw that climbing gear, I was pretty sure it was mine," Bryan said, speaking rapidly in a low voice. "So when I got home from work Friday morning, I checked my Jeep, where I leave my gear. Someone had sliced through the canvas top of my Jeep and stolen my equipment." Bryan looked from Nancy to Ned to George and back to Nancy again. He sounded a little desperate as he continued. "Don't you see? The thief used my equipment to break into the museum."

"Where do you park your Jeep?" Nancy asked.

"Behind Omega Chi, and at the museum when I'm working."

"Did you report the break-in to the police?" Nancy watched Bryan carefully.

"No."

"Why not?" George cried, putting her hand on his shoulder and forcing him to meet her eyes.

"Who'd have believed me?" Bryan challenged. "Put two and two together. I was locked in a shed while *my* climbing gear was used to rob the museum. Sooner or later the police would have to conclude I was the thief. My friends don't believe me—why should the cops?"

"You've got a point," Ned said grimly.

"You have to tell the police," Nancy said firmly. Ripping a sheet out of her notebook, she copied down Sergeant Weinberg's number for Bryan. Reluctantly he took it and put it in his pocket.

After paying the bill, they silently trooped out to the parking lot. Bryan showed Nancy the slit in the black canvas top of his Jeep. Not sure what she was looking for, Nancy examined the tear.

Bryan seemed to be telling the truth. But he could have slashed the top himself to support his story.

George rode back to campus with Bryan, and Nancy and Ned headed back alone. Neither of them felt like talking. When Ned got out of the car in front of Omega Chi, he walked around to Nancy's open window and leaned in. He cupped her chin in his hand. "Nan, I'm worried about Bryan, too," he said softly, "but I trust you. If Bryan's guilty, you'll prove it. But if he's innocent, you'll find the real thief and he'll be in the clear." Ned kissed the tip of Nancy's nose. He smiled, but the expression in his eyes was a little sad. "You look tired," he said tenderly. "Even great detectives need their sleep."

Parking the Mustang in the Theta Pi driveway a few minutes later, Nancy looked for Debbie's white Subaru. It wasn't in the lot, and there was no light on in her bedroom. Were Debbie and her mystery friend still out together? If so, where?

That night Nancy fell asleep thinking about her next moves. She had to search Bryan's room and confront Debbie about that girl.

"Nancy, wake up." George shook her hard.

Nancy opened her eyes. The light was dazzling and George was smiling. Nancy rubbed her eyes with her fists. "What's up?"

"Someone phoned Debbie. The person left *First Kiss* in the college chapel. She said she'll meet us there."

Nancy was already in motion. After pulling on jeans and a T-shirt, she dialed Sergeant Weinberg and relayed the information.

Debbie was already at the chapel searching behind the altar. Sun flooded through the stained-glass windows casting a red and blue glow on Debbie's blond hair. "Who called?" Nancy asked.

"I don't know—I couldn't tell if it was a man or a woman. The person said the painting was here and hung up." Debbie seemed frantic.

"We'll split up to search," Nancy directed.

Nancy took the front, George the side aisles, Debbie the back. Within minutes Nancy spied something under the third pew. She reached for the package and tore off the brown paper. "I found it!"

She held the painting up to the light and caught her breath. Michael must have really loved this girl, she thought.

"Why did someone steal it just to bring it back?" George asked. She stared quietly at the painting. "It's wonderful. It's what being in love feels like," George said.

"I don't believe this." Debbie touched the painting with reverence. "This whole awful nightmare is finally over."

As the three girls were gazing at *First Kiss,* Sergeant Weinberg rushed in. Nancy handed him the painting.

Nancy sat down in the first pew, staring at the colorful mural above the altar. Stealing a painting only to return it made no sense—unless Nancy was closing in on the culprit and whoever it was was panicking. Nancy had turned up the heat on just one suspect so far: Bryan.

As Sergeant Weinberg interviewed Debbie, Nancy listened intently, hoping for a new lead. But Debbie only repeated her story of the anonymous caller.

"I'll return the painting to the museum immediately," the police sergeant told the girls.

"Isn't it wonderful? The painting is back. Now you can stop investigating." Debbie flashed Nancy a sunny smile.

"No way." Nancy slid out of the pew. "The painting's back, but a crime was committed. And I'm going to keep looking for the thief." Nancy watched Debbie's smile fade.

"You drove away from the Theta Pi house Saturday morning with a blond girl in your car, Debbie," Nancy pressed on. "The same girl who posed as Kate Robertson in Michael's class. You lied when I asked about her before. Who is she?"

Silence.

"Who is she?" Nancy repeated.

"I can't tell you, Nancy." Debbie's voice dropped to a whisper. "But I swear she's got nothing to do with *First Kiss.*" After turning abruptly, Debbie ran out of the chapel.

"I've never been to an opening before," Ned confessed to Nancy that afternoon. "Are they always this crowded?" he asked, looking around the contemporary art gallery of the Emerson museum.

"Michael's pretty famous," Nancy reminded him. "And all that publicity about the theft probably helped draw a crowd."

"Amazing how many people are dressed in black." Ned looked down at his own tan slacks and teal blue tie.

"Makes you feel sort of out of place." Nancy giggled and touched the skirt of her long floral print dress. "Michael's fashionable friends from New York must have turned up. They always wear black."

"None of them compares with you," Ned whispered. "You're the most beautiful girl in the room."

Nancy colored with pleasure and took Ned's hand between both of hers. "Not quite," she said and pulled him over to the far wall where the throng of people was thickest. "Look at her." Nancy pointed to the girl in *First Kiss*.

Ned studied it. "I don't know much about art," he admitted, "but it's a beautiful painting. No wonder someone stole it."

"But why did he or she bring it back in time for the opening, Ned?" Nancy asked in a low voice as they headed for the buffet table to get a soda.

Near the gallery entrance Nancy spotted George and Bryan. They were talking with Ian

Sanders. Nancy was surprised to see Rina hovering near them. But then she realized Rina's white jacket and black pants was a uniform. Rina was working for the campus food service catering the event.

Ned tapped her elbow and handed her a cola. "I wonder if she got her job back." Nancy followed his eyes. Debbie was standing next to *First Kiss*, taking in the crowd. She seemed to be excited and looked very pretty in a pale pink suit.

"Dr. Morrison has no reason not to hire her back—unless of course we find out she's the thief after all."

"Nan, you don't really believe that?"

Nancy laughed. "Honestly? No. But I can't completely rule her out. We've only her word about the anonymous phone call. Maybe she returned the painting—maybe she figured I found some other incriminating evidence in her room the other day. . . ." Nancy paused to think. She was pretty sure she had left the room exactly as she had found it.

Suddenly a light round of applause rippled through the gallery. Nancy peered over Ned's shoulder to watch Michael walk in. He was dressed in his usual black T-shirt and black jeans. He looked right past Nancy because he had eyes only for his painting. He finally stopped in front of *First Kiss*.

Nancy watched his face light up in an incredible smile. He seemed to drink in every detail of the painting. Then his expression changed abruptly. His back stiffened. He swayed and grabbed the nearest person, Debbie. Clutching her arm, he cried, "This is not my *First Kiss*. This painting is a forgery!"

Chapter

Eleven

THE SILENCE that greeted Michael's outburst was complete. When the gallery finally exploded with sound, the noise was deafening. Everyone pushed forward to see the forgery up close.

Michael seemed to be stunned as he stood stock still holding on to Debbie's arm. Finally his eyes sought out Nancy, who dropped Ned's hand and hurried to Michael's side.

"Nancy!" Michael grabbed both of Nancy's hands. "Tell me this isn't happening. . . ."

Nancy felt terrible for him as her mind was madly trying to fit in this new piece of the puzzle. "Michael, this is awful, but you must think," she urged. "Who would—no, who *could* do this?"

Michael appeared to be confused. "Someone very good," he said finally. He made Nancy face the painting. "The forgery is almost perfect.

Hardly anyone would be able to tell but me." He pointed to a spot where the blond girl's hair blended into the shadowy background. Several thin gold brush strokes stood out. "I never use line like that."

"What do we do now?" Debbie's voice jarred Nancy. The color had drained from Debbie's face, and she looked as if she were going to faint.

Michael noticed her for the first time. "Aren't you Debbie Lakin?"

"We've met before. At the art contest—I was the student judge. And I—I used to work here. I'm so upset. When we found the painting today in the chapel, I thought your troubles were over."

Nancy observed Debbie carefully. *Used to work here.* So Morrison hadn't hired her back. "Michael," Nancy assured him, "I'm going to find the original. I promise."

People stepped up to talk to Michael, and Debbie blended back into the crowd. Nancy searched for Ned. She spotted Dr. Morrison near Michael. He was livid. Who could blame him? The forgery was a terrible embarrassment for him. Despite his expertise, he'd been taken in by a forgery.

Nancy noticed Rina breezing around the gallery, serving drinks from a tray. Her red ponytail swung behind her, and she had a giant smirk on her face. Did Rina hate them so much that she'd laugh at this disaster? Or did that smile mean even more?

Rina wasn't the only one enjoying the situation. Nancy noticed Ian Sanders actually grinning as he studied the forged painting.

She finally found Ned in the museum garden sitting on a metal bench and nursing his soda.

He raised his head as she approached. "Sometimes I think a guy's got to be in trouble for you to notice him."

Nancy felt a pang of guilt. "Now, Nickerson, this case just got a lot more interesting."

"For once I understand." He patted the seat next to him, but Nancy chose to sit on his lap. She wrapped her arms around his neck and lost herself a moment in the clean soapy smell of his hair. "You're a very distracting person," she murmured as they shared a kiss.

A few moments later she shifted to the bench and leaned her head against his shoulder. The afternoon was hot and muggy, and Nancy guessed it would rain soon. "A forgery," Nancy mused. "That explains why the painting was returned."

"What nerve—the forger actually believed he or she could fool the artist," Ned said.

"The thief may have been overly confident," Nancy agreed, "and believed the forgery wouldn't be discovered. With the heat off, they could sell the original. An unscrupulous collector wouldn't hesitate to buy stolen work."

"What's your next move, Nan?" Ned asked.

Nancy smiled. "Actually, the forgery may help

us. We know the thief's an experienced climber and is probably in cahoots with a top-notch artist. That should narrow the field."

"Any ideas?"

"Yes," Nancy replied. "I told you about Kate Robertson's copy of the *Mona Lisa*. It's *good*. Kate is supposed to be in Paris, but maybe she's back. I know Debbie's hiding the blond girl, but maybe she's got Kate stashed, too."

"You think the three of them are working together?" Ned asked.

"Could be," Nancy replied. "It's possible that Debbie or Kate or the blond girl stole the painting and Kate copied it, but then one of them would have to know how to rappel down a rope into the museum. It's even more likely that Debbie and Bryan worked together to steal the painting, still using Kate, with Bryan actually committing the robbery."

Ned grimaced at the mention of Bryan's involvement. "What about the blond girl?" he asked.

"She could be involved, too," Nancy explained. "And there's another possibility— Rina. Rina may be a good enough painter to produce that forgery. Her ushering assignment isn't a foolproof alibi."

"But the EC ticket stub you found on the roof," Ned countered. "If Rina ushered for the EC concert, why would she have had a ticket stub?"

"She wouldn't," Nancy said.

"If Rina is the thief, that at least would take Bryan out of the picture," Ned declared.

"Not necessarily," Nancy said. "Rina got Bryan his job at the museum. He and Rina could have plotted to steal the painting, using Debbie as a pawn to gain access to the museum art."

"I can't believe Bryan would do that."

"We have to consider all possibilities," Nancy cautioned. "And don't forget Morrison. He's got an alibi for the time of the theft, but he could have an accomplice and be the mastermind. Like Rina, he seems to need money."

"Dr. Morrison knows Ian Sanders," Ned said. "Maybe he's planning to sell him the painting."

"Or maybe Bryan is planning to sell the painting to Sanders," Nancy added.

"Hey!" George called out as she and Bryan strolled into the courtyard. "We've been looking all over for you two. Everyone's starting to leave."

Bryan shifted uneasily as he stood in front of Nancy. They hadn't spoken since dinner the night before. "This morning I spoke with Sergeant Weinberg about my stolen gear." Bryan seemed depressed. "I was pretty scared about losing my job until I heard the painting was returned. Now I guess I'm back in the hot seat again."

"I'm hungry," Ned said, changing the subject.

"Pizza?" George suggested.

"Oh, yeah!" Ned exclaimed happily.

Nancy wanted to freshen up before they went out to eat. "I'll meet you in front of the museum," she told her friends.

Five minutes later Nancy was leaving the women's rest room when she heard voices at the end of the hall where the storage room was located. "Yes, the paintings are quite nice," a resonant male voice said, "but as you know, I'm only interested in Jared's work these days."

Nancy stepped back behind the rest room door, hoping to hear more. All she heard, though, were footsteps passing by. When she popped her head out again, she saw Dr. Morrison with Ian Sanders walking toward the museum lobby. Nancy followed them. Was Sanders fishing to buy the stolen painting? she wondered.

Nancy paused as Dr. Morrison stopped to place a set of keys in the receptionist's desk. He looked up. "Nancy! I thought everyone had gone. I was just showing Mr. Sanders some of the paintings the museum will be selling hoping to persuade him to buy something." Dr. Morrison introduced Nancy to Sanders. "Nancy is a detective investigating the theft of *First Kiss.*"

Nancy winced. She would have preferred that Ian Sanders not know she was working on the case. Sanders smiled coolly. "A pleasure, Nancy."

"That was a hilarious movie," George announced as she and Nancy walked into the sorority house later that night. "I'm glad Bryan suggested it."

Nancy agreed. After pizza the four had stopped to see a new comedy that kept them in stitches.

George had already started up the stairs when the house phone rang. No one seemed to be answering it. "I'll get it." Nancy hurried to pick it up.

The caller was a Mrs. Shephard calling for Debbie. "It's urgent," Mrs. Shephard's gravelly voice declared.

"Just a moment please," Nancy said. She ran to the house intercom to announce the call for Debbie. Halfway through her announcement Nancy saw the back door open. Debbie started to come in, but then she stepped back.

Hadn't Debbie heard her name on the intercom? "Debbie!" No one answered.

With a groan Nancy took a message from Mrs. Shephard. "I've been trying to contact Debbie for two days," the woman complained, "but she hasn't returned my calls." After hanging up, Nancy copied down Mrs. Shephard's number in her notebook, then wrote out the message for Debbie.

Nancy was puzzled. Who was Mrs. Shephard, and why was Debbie avoiding her?

Chapter

Twelve

As Nancy tacked the message on the call board, she heard giggling in the den. Maybe the girls could tell her something about Mrs. Shephard. Inside, Mindy, Chris, and Brook were watching home videos and munching popcorn.

Two girls dressed as clowns were on the TV screen. "The tall clown is me." Chris smiled up at Nancy. "The other clown is Debbie. We put on some skits for the girls from a halfway house this summer when they came to see the museum."

In the next segment sorority sisters played tug-of-war with a line of younger girls.

Nancy sat on the arm of the couch. "Sorry to interrupt, but who's Mrs. Shephard? She phoned just now and seemed anxious to talk to Debbie."

Brook stopped the video. "Great timing, Nancy. Here's Mrs. Shephard." At the end of the girls' tug-of-war line was a small middle-aged woman in shorts. "She runs the McKinleyville halfway house," Brook explained, restarting the video.

"Stop!" Nancy cried. Brook froze the screen. In the line of young girls Nancy saw the tall girl with long stringy brown hair. The shot wasn't a closeup, but Nancy was sure she was Debbie's friend—the girl who had stolen the art packet at the bookstore. "Who's the tall girl?"

Chris looked at Brook. "What's her name?"

"Jamie," Mindy piped up. "I remember her because she painted those cool horses in Debbie's room."

"Could you replay that clown sequence?" Nancy asked excitedly. She knew she was onto something. As the video images flashed by, Nancy caught several glimpses of Jamie, though none close up.

Nancy's mind clicked away. Why had Debbie denied knowing Jamie? Did Debbie know that Jamie stole the art supplies? Nancy remembered the drawing she found in Debbie's room. Was Jamie the artist behind the forgery? Nancy's mind raced. She decided she had to find Jamie and talk to Mrs. Shephard. She'd never get a straight answer from Debbie.

Early the next morning Nancy called Mrs. Shephard. Until she knew more about Jamie and the halfway house, she decided it would be best to keep Mrs. Shephard in the dark about her investigation. "I'm calling from Emerson College," Nancy told her. "I'm writing an article for the college paper about your halfway house. Could a friend and I visit you today? It won't take long," Nancy promised.

Mrs. Shephard hesitated, then said, "Sure. Come on out. I like people to learn about us."

Ten minutes later Nancy and George were heading for McKinleyville. "Looks like rain," George commented, peering out the window. Nancy agreed. She couldn't wait for the heat wave to break.

The halfway house was a small brick building that resembled an old school. Mrs. Shephard met them at the door. Despite the woman's firm handshake and warm smile, Nancy could see the tension and fatigue in her eyes.

Nancy and George followed Mrs. Shephard into her office. After they were seated, Nancy began by saying she needed some general background on the halfway house for her article. Mrs. Shephard seemed eager to answer. Every so often George commented on the house. Then, feeling the moment was right, Nancy honed in on the special classes offered to the runaway girls, like Debbie's art class over the summer.

At the mention of Debbie's name, Mrs. Shephard became wary.

"We like to expose the girls to as many different experiences as possible," Mrs. Shephard said, "like the museum art class."

George nodded enthusiastically. "Debbie

never stops talking about how much she loved teaching that class," George said. "Wasn't there some really gifted kid in that class?

Nancy pretended to think, then riffled through her notebook. "Yes—here it is. Jamie." Nancy looked up. "Is she around? I'd love to interview her."

Mrs. Shephard stiffened. "You can't."

"Why not?" Nancy asked.

"Jamie's not here."

"Where is she?" Nancy snapped her notebook shut. "I could interview her somewhere else."

Mrs. Shephard's face sagged. "Jamie ran away. I'm terribly worried. I don't want to bring in the police unless I have to. These kids trust me." She motioned Nancy to sit back down. "Kids come here through a helpline—generally they just need time away from their own homes. But Jamie's been gone since Thursday morning. Jamie's roommate told me that Jamie talked of spending the weekend at Emerson. But it's Monday, and she's not back yet."

There was a knock on the door. A young woman entered, asking if she could speak to Mrs. Shephard privately for a moment. Mrs. Shephard rose and said, "Excuse me for a moment. I'll be right back."

"Watch the door, George," Nancy directed the minute Mrs. Shephard was out of the room. With George on guard, Nancy scanned the papers on the desk for any clue that might explain Jamie's connection to the case.

Near the top of one pile of papers, Nancy found a folder labeled Jamie Peters. Inside was a photograph of a young girl. "George, it's the girl in the bookstore."

As Nancy studied the photo more closely, something bothered her. Then she had it. Nancy realized she had seen this girl *after* the shoplifting incident. Why hadn't she noticed before? All the time the evidence of who she was had been staring right at her. The hair was dramatically different, but the face was the same. Jamie was the girl with blond spiky hair who was masquerading as Kate.

"Hurry, Nancy," George whispered. "She's coming."

Quickly Nancy closed the file and sat down primly in her seat.

"Thank you for your patience, girls," Mrs. Shephard said. "How else can I help you?"

Nancy stood up and shook hands with Mrs. Shephard. "You've helped us a lot. When Jamie does come back here, I'd love to speak with her," Nancy said.

"Don't worry," George added. "I know Debbie. Jamie couldn't be in better hands. . . ."

"If she's with Debbie. I only wish Debbie would return my calls."

"If we run into Jamie, we'll give you a call right away," Nancy promised.

George had a lunch date with Bryan, so Nancy dropped her off near the student union. After returning to the sorority house, Nancy knocked on Debbie's door. Debbie opened it cautiously, frowning when she saw Nancy. "We have to talk," Nancy said. "I know about Jamie."

Debbie gave a little cry, covering her face with her hands. Nancy pushed by her and went into the room.

"You've been hiding Jamie," Nancy continued, standing with her hands on her hips.

"No," Debbie began. "You've got it all wrong."

"I don't think so," Nancy said evenly. "I've been to McKinleyville. I've seen Jamie's file. Jamie's been masquerading as Kate."

A sigh escaped Debbie.

"You're in enough trouble as it is," Nancy told her softly. "The only way I can help you is by hearing the truth."

Debbie looked up with tears in her eyes. She nodded. "I found Jamie hiding in the museum storage room the night of the robbery. I'd left the door unlocked because I'd been going in and out. She sneaked in, looking for a hiding place."

"That was about the time the theft occurred."

"Yes," Debbie said. "Oh, Nancy, that's why I didn't know the robbery was happening. I was trying to convince Jamie to go back to the halfway house when we heard the police siren. Jamie got scared and climbed out the window."

"She came here that night," Nancy said. "That's who I saw throwing pebbles."

"Yes," Debbie admitted.

"Why did Jamie go to the museum in the first place?"

"To see Michael Jared's work," Debbie explained. "That's why I feel so responsible for her running away. I showed the girls slides of his paintings this past summer, and Jamie fell in love with them."

"I saw Jamie shoplifting," Nancy said, sitting down on the bottom bunk.

"I know." Debbie paced the room as she talked. "It was wrong, and I told her she had to put the packet back. But she had opened it already. I took what was left and put it in Kate's footlocker. I couldn't figure out how to return it without getting Jamie into trouble."

"So that's what you meant when you said 'put it back.' I overheard you on the phone that day. You were talking to Jamie." Suddenly she had a thought. "Your slashed dress?" Nancy asked.

Debbie stood up, wringing her hands. "I think Jamie did that. She was mad because I confronted her and told her to go back to the halfway house. I think she needs help. But she's not a bad kid. Not really."

"And Kate's registration packet?" Nancy thought rapidly. "Isn't that how Jamie knew Kate was registered for Michael's drawing class?"

Debbie nodded.

"Then after the bookstore theft, Jamie changed her appearance."

"A beauty school was offering makeovers," Debbie said. Nancy remembered the flyer someone handed her Friday afternoon. "Maybe she thought someone besides you saw her. Maybe she was scared Mrs. Shephard would call the police and they'd recognize her from a picture. I don't know." Debbie sank down on the bunk next to Nancy, burying her head in her arms. "This has been the worst couple of days."

Nancy felt sorry for her and was sure now Debbie had nothing to do with the robbery. "You've got to call Mrs. Shephard and get Jamie to go back to the halfway house before Mrs. Shephard does call in the police."

"I'll try to talk to her one more time," Debbie said. "She needs to go back to McKinleyville, but if she's forced to go back against her will, she'll just run away again."

Just then Nancy heard a noise. The window behind the drawn curtains was being raised. Both she and Debbie froze. A slender arm parted the curtains. A girl with spiky blond hair poked her head through.

"Hello, Jamie," Nancy said calmly.

Jamie's mouth dropped open as she stared at Nancy. Then she ducked back out the window.

"Jamie!" Debbie cried. Nancy dashed out of the room, and through the kitchen into the yard. She spotted Jamie racing down the street and started after her, Debbie on her heels. The two girls chased the runaway down to Main Street, where she ducked into a small shopping arcade.

Nancy and Debbie tore through the arched entrance, but Jamie was gone. "We lost her!" Debbie wailed.

"Keep looking," Nancy ordered her firmly. "You're the only one Jamie will listen to." Nancy watched Debbie disappear into the crowded arcade. Nancy believed Debbie was telling the truth, which meant she had nothing to do with the theft. That left Bryan as the prime suspect. Nancy remembered that Bryan had a dinner date with Ian Sanders that night. Maybe Bryan stole the painting for Sanders. Nancy had to find it before they met tonight. Bryan and George were having lunch now, so this was her chance to search his room. Nancy needed to call Ned to ask for his help.

Back at Theta Pi, Nancy headed toward the house phone. Rina's roommate, Terri Beck, was just hanging up the receiver. She looked upset. "What's wrong?" Nancy asked.

"Rina didn't come home last night," Terri replied. "And she didn't show up for her shift at the café this morning. Rina's difficult, but she's very responsible. She never misses work. I'm worried."

Rina's disappearance was suspicious, Nancy thought. "Where does Rina usually hang out?" Nancy asked.

"I don't know," Terri answered. "Rina doesn't share her personal life with me, or anyone."

Nancy felt pulled in two directions—she wanted to find Rina, but Bryan's room had to be

119

searched. Nodding goodbye to Terri, she dialed Omega Chi. Ned answered the phone. "I just walked in the door," he said. "What's up?"

Nancy briefed Ned and he immediately agreed to help. Nancy was grateful because she knew this was painful for Ned. Bryan was a friend.

When Nancy arrived at Omega Chi, Ned told her that Bryan shared a room with Howie Little at the end of the second-floor hall. "Howie's working on his car in the parking lot, so make it fast, Nan," Ned cautioned. With Ned standing lookout, Nancy bounded up the stairs. The room wasn't locked.

Half the room was neat, the other half a mess. Ned had told her Howie was a slob. Starting on the neat side, Nancy searched the drawers, the bedding, the closets. She even tested for loose floorboards. *First Kiss* wasn't in the room.

Dejected, Nancy rejoined Ned. "Where else would Bryan keep his things?" she asked.

"We have lockers for extras in the garage," Ned said.

"So let's go." On their way to the garage, Howie Little waved hello, then ducked back under the hood of his car. A raindrop fell on Nancy's nose. She glanced up and saw the sky darkening.

Ned unlocked the combination lock on the garage door. A vintage convertible was parked on one side. The rest of the place was filled with old furniture. A bank of lockers hugged one wall.

"Ned," Howie called. "I need your help."

"I'll just be a minute," Ned promised.

With no time to waste Nancy scanned the names on the lockers until she came to *Barbour*. She heard Ned behind her. "I'll hurry," she whispered.

Suddenly someone grabbed her arm, jerked her around, and shoved her back against the bank of metal lockers. Nancy looked up into Bryan Barbour's angry green eyes.

Chapter

Thirteen

WHAT ARE YOU DOING looking at my locker?" Bryan bellowed. "I reported my gear stolen. My job's probably on the line now. What more do you want?"

Nancy let her body go limp, and Bryan loosened his hold. Seizing her moment, Nancy squirmed out of his reach.

"What's going on here?" George cried, walking into the garage. Ned was right behind her.

"Nothing," Nancy said quickly. She turned to Bryan. "If you're innocent, then you won't mind if I check your locker."

"Be my guest," Bryan said, and opened it. Inside was a skateboard, boxing gloves, and a tennis racket.

"Satisfied?" Bryan asked.

"Thank you." Nancy closed the locker.

Bryan noticed Ned. "You think I'm a thief, too?"

"No, but Nancy has to investigate everyone."

George moved to Bryan's side. "Haven't you got enough proof now?" she said to Nancy. "He's innocent."

Nancy felt terrible, but she had to tell the truth. "I don't know that yet."

Brian groaned. "I told you. I've been framed. Someone wants it to look like I stole *First Kiss.*"

"So you claim. But who'd frame you?"

"I'm not accusing anybody, but there's only one person I know who'd want to hurt me and that's Rina."

"You think Rina stole your equipment and robbed the museum?"

"I don't know," Bryan said, his expression troubled. "Especially now with the forgery, I just don't know. Rina wouldn't do a copy again."

"What do you mean 'again'?" Nancy suddenly felt a prickly sensation at the back of her neck. Could this be the lead she'd been waiting for?

"Rina's done copies before. She's fantastic at it. When an exhibit from the Morgan Museum in Vancouver came to Emerson last spring, she copied some paintings. They were good enough for the museum gift shop to sell as reproductions. Even Dr. Morrison asked her to copy a picture in the Morgan exhibit for him. But after that, she stopped. She told me she'd never do a copy again."

"Did she say why?" Nancy asked.

"No," Bryan replied. "But Rina's really determined to paint in her own style—so maybe that's why she's not interested in copies. She wouldn't talk about it."

"Has Rina done any climbing?" Nancy probed, trying not to sound too excited. "Could she lower herself into the museum?"

"Sure," Bryan said. "We used to climb a lot in high school, back in Colorado."

"Rina didn't return to her room last night," Nancy told him. "Any idea where she is?"

Bryan thought for a moment. "Rina's aunt has a cabin out in Lincoln Valley. Rina used to go there to paint and be alone."

"Can you give me directions?" Nancy asked.

"Yeah." Bryan scribbled in the notebook Nancy took out of her backpack.

"I should go with you, Nan," Ned said.

"Don't be silly. What could Rina possibly do to me? Don't you have to study?" Nancy said lightly.

"I'll come," Bryan offered.

Nancy shook her head sharply. "No. Rina hates you. I won't be able to get a thing out of her with you around."

George glanced at Bryan and then back at Nancy. "I'm game," she volunteered.

"I'd like to stop at the museum before we go to Lincoln Valley," Nancy told George after she waved goodbye to Ned and Bryan. The rain was coming down steadily as they crossed the Theta Pi lot and climbed into Nancy's Mustang.

"You want to check on Bryan's story about Rina."

Nancy tried to ignore the disappointment in George's voice. "I have to. But I think he's telling the truth," she said.

Nancy parked the car. "I'll be right back." Nancy dashed through the rain into the museum. Dr. Morrison was in his office, studying computer printouts. He looked up with bleary eyes when she knocked on the open door.

"Good news?" he asked expectantly.

"Not yet," Nancy said. "But I've got some questions about Rina. I understand she did a copy of a painting for you last spring."

"Why, yes, she did," Dr. Morrison replied, obviously surprised by the question. "It was of a painting that was here on loan."

"Could Rina have forged *First Kiss*?"

Dr. Morrison's eyes glinted. "Yes. I'd say so." He paused. "So you're suggesting Rina—"

"I'm not suggesting anything right now," Nancy cut in. "I'm just asking questions." She turned to go. "Excuse me, Dr. Morrison. I have to run.

On the way to Lincoln Valley the rain picked up until sheets of water cascaded over the windshield. Nancy had to lean forward over the steering wheel to see the road.

"So Dr. Morrison thinks Rina is good enough

125

to have forged *First Kiss,*" George commented, wiping the fog off the inside of the windshield with her sleeve.

"Right. But don't forget Dr. Morrison is a suspect, too. Still, he confirmed Bryan's story about Rina." Nancy turned down a dirt road that was a muddy mess. "Are you sure Bryan said to turn here?" she asked doubtfully.

"That's what the directions say," George assured her, reading from the piece of paper she held. "After the gas station, go right on the first dirt road."

Nancy concentrated on her driving. The road grew muddier by the second, and the car jerked and swerved as Nancy expertly maneuvered around huge ruts. Then the road turned left, away from a bridge that would take them across a swollen river. It wound through fields beside the river. Nancy hoped they wouldn't get lost.

Finally a blue farmhouse came into sight. It was just as Bryan had described. About two miles past it, they glimpsed a cabin set back from the road. "That's it!" Nancy said, spotting Rina's green sedan out front.

Nancy was surprised to see smoke rising from the cabin's chimney—though rainy, the day was warm. "I'm going to park by the road," Nancy told George. "It looks like we could get stuck in that driveway."

The girls raced up a stone path toward the cabin. Nancy peeked in the front window. Rina stood in front of the fireplace, throwing scraps of paper into the flames.

"What's she doing?" George gasped. Nancy raced inside, George right behind her.

"Oh!" Rina cried, frightened. Then she looked down at the last paper in her hands and tossed it into the fireplace.

Before the flames touched it, Nancy bounded over to the fireplace and pulled it out. It was a drawing of *First Kiss*. Nancy looked straight at Rina. "Is this a preliminary sketch? Did you forge *First Kiss*?"

Rina froze.

"Did you steal the painting, Rina?"

Rina started to shake, and Nancy had her answer. "I was going to return it," Rina said. Rina's voice, like her body, was quivering.

"Where's the original now?" Nancy grilled her.

"I don't know!" Rina cried. "It was in the trunk of my car. I was going to return it to the museum after they discovered the copy, I swear. But someone stole it from my car. That's why I got so scared and ran away. Somebody knows what I did and stole the painting. Now I can't return it!"

"But why did you do it?" George asked bewildered.

"I—I just wanted to prove a point," Rina stammered.

"What point?" Nancy was incredulous.

127

Rina's face changed, her fear transformed to anger. "They thought I wasn't good enough to win the college art contest," she said, her voice growing stronger. "I overheard Morrison describe my entry as primitive, awkward. Of course my work looks primitive!" Rina exclaimed. "It's deliberate. But the three judges—Debbie, Dr. Morrison, Michael Jared—thought I wasn't talented enough to win the contest. I should have won. I needed that prize. It was a full scholarship to Emerson. Without it I won't have enough to graduate."

"So you were getting back at them?" George asked, trying hard to understand.

"I was going to show them," Rina responded feverishly. "I can paint in any style I want, even Michael Jared's. I was going to show them, and I did." Rina seemed crazed with spite.

"But I made sure Michael would recognize the painting as a forgery," she went on, a nasty gleam in her eyes. "You see, I made little changes, changes that Debbie and Dr. Morrison wouldn't notice. But Michael would. Debbie and Dr. Morrison were embarrassed—just as I planned."

Nancy gripped Rina's hands. "Do you know who took the painting?" she asked.

"No!" Rina cried, breaking away. "You've got to believe me."

The door opened, and a tall red-haired woman of about fifty walked in. "Terrible rain." The woman shook the water off her slicker. Her resemblance to Rina was striking. "You didn't tell me we were having guests."

Glowering, Rina introduced her aunt Rae.

"Would you like coffee or tea?" Rae asked.

Nancy shook her head. "We've got to get back." Nancy asked Rina to walk them to the car.

Outside Nancy took Rina by the arm, gripping her tightly. She stood under the dripping eaves of the house. "Was Bryan in on the theft?" Nancy asked. She heard George catch her breath beside her.

"No," Rina admitted. "I stole his gear."

"He could lose his job because of you." George spoke sharply.

Rina's eyes were cold. "Fine by me. He deserved it."

Nancy winced. "You were ushering that night. How did you pull off the robbery?"

"It wasn't hard," Rina explained. "I skated most of the way to the museum after the second intermission. Then I took off my skates and ran up the hill. There was just enough time to get back to the theater before the play let out."

In her mind Nancy saw the hooded skater racing across campus that first night. "So that was you," Nancy said. "I saw you that night— you bumped into me. You had the painting then."

Rina nodded. "I had it in my pack. I skated to my car and put my pack in the trunk. Then I ran back to the theater. No one knew I'd been gone."

"You stuffed *First Kiss* into a backpack?" Nancy asked incredulously.

"I wrapped it up in a sweatshirt first." Rina was defensive. "I didn't damage it."

"What about the ticket stub?" George asked. "Nancy found an EC ticket stub on the roof."

"I don't know anything about that," Rina said.

"I have to report all this to Sergeant Weinberg," Nancy told Rina. "But it would be better for you if you turned yourself in."

Rina gazed down at her muddy boots and nodded her head. "I guess I have no choice. Nobody will understand," she said bitterly. Nancy hoped Rina made her confession quickly. She was in big trouble, and she had to face up to it.

"At least Bryan's in the clear." George gave a big sigh of relief. As they got into the Mustang, Nancy said nothing. Bryan might be in the clear about the museum theft, but they didn't know who had *First Kiss* now. Bryan could have it, or even Rina, if she had lied about it having been stolen from her car.

The drive back was terrible. The rain had turned the potholes to ponds, and Nancy could barely avoid running the Mustang into a ditch. Swerving, she barely avoided a bale of hay that had rolled onto the road.

Just ahead Nancy saw a bridge and wondered if she'd taken a wrong turn. Hadn't they turned before the bridge on the way out? "Is this the right way?" Nancy asked, moving onto the bridge.

"Nancy, look!" George screamed, and a bolt of terror shot up Nancy's spine. A few yards ahead the bridge abruptly ended. The drop off from it was about thirty feet down—straight into the raging river!

Nancy jammed on the brake, and the car swerved uncontrollably.

Chapter

Fourteen

THE MUSTANG FISHTAILED, slamming into the metal guardrails. Struggling to control the car, Nancy caught flashes of the river below and the drop-off ahead. She finally steered into the skid, and the Mustang hit the railing head on. It bounced across to the other guardrail, then back again. Finally the car came to a stop.

Nancy turned off the ignition, her hands trembling. "You okay?" she whispered.

"Yeah," George said in a small voice. "I'd call that a little scary, even for us, Nan."

"Very scary," Nancy echoed. The two girls sat in silence a moment. Then, very cautiously, Nancy tried her door. Her stomach lurched when she saw that they had missed the end of the bridge by inches.

When the rain let up, Nancy climbed out and

surveyed the damage to her car. The sides were scraped, and one headlight and Nancy's door were bashed in. George got out and checked for damage, too. "Bad luck," she said.

"More than bad luck," Nancy replied. "Where are the signs saying the bridge is out? And where are the barricades across the entrance? Let's look." It wasn't long before Nancy and George found the warning signs and barricades stowed in nearby bushes. Someone had deliberately hidden them.

Just then a black-and-white highway patrol car pulled up. A state trooper leaped out. "You girls all right?" he asked.

After assuring the officer they were, Nancy briefed him on the incident. "I was afraid of that," he said soberly. "When I drove by the first turnoff on the highway just now, I noticed there was no danger sign. I drove down here to check on the detour sign and barricades." He shook his head in disgust. "Probably kids playing a joke."

The officer took down their names and the details of the incident before giving the girls directions back to Emerson.

"I have the feeling someone who knew we were heading out to Lincoln Valley didn't want us to come back," Nancy told George as she backed the car off the bridge. The officer waited to be sure they were okay. Nancy waved to him, and he took off. George stared straight ahead. Only Ned and Bryan knew they were going to Lincoln

Valley. Ned was above suspicion. So that left Bryan. . . .

On the ride back Nancy kept returning to the same questions. If Bryan had figured out that Rina had been responsible for the theft and the forgery, could he have stolen the original from Rina? And were the missing signs and barricades at the bridge supposed to keep Nancy from revealing Bryan's secret?

At the sorority house Nancy immediately went up to the room she was sharing with Chris and called Ned. Hearing his voice, Nancy almost burst into tears. The stress of the accident had really gotten to her. Playing down the seriousness of the incident, she filled Ned in on what had happened.

Ned gave Bryan an alibi. "Bryan left a half hour ago to walk over to dinner with Ian Sanders," Ned explained. "But Bryan's been at the house all afternoon working."

"Was he carrying anything when he left?"

"Nothing," Ned replied. "I have to be at the house for another half hour, but if you need me I'll come right now." He paused. "I don't want anything to happen to you, Nancy."

"Not necessary, Ned," Nancy answered gently, "but I appreciate the offer. George will be with me. If we need reinforcements, I know where to find you." After hanging up, Nancy lay back on the bed. If Bryan was in the clear, who had sabotaged the bridge?

Dr. Morrison. Nancy sat straight up. Dr. Morrison hadn't known where Nancy was headed that afternoon, but he had known she was looking for Rina. If Rina had copied a drawing for him once, then he might guess that Rina had forged *First Kiss.* Could he have stolen the original from Rina's car?

Why would he try to harm Nancy and George, though? That last part only made sense if Dr. Morrison felt threatened by Nancy. And he had no reason to feel threatened—yet. Besides, how could he have known about Rina's aunt's cabin or that the girls were driving there? Nancy shook her head to clear it. She was missing an important piece of the puzzle.

The phone rang. It was Mindy, forwarding a call from the house phone. Carson Drew's deep voice came on Nancy's line. "I've got information on Geoffrey Morrison," he told her.

Nancy smiled. "Your timing's perfect, Dad."

"I spoke with a member of the Cabbott board of directors," he began. "What I'm about to tell you is very hush-hush. No accusations were ever made, but there was suspicion."

"I'm dying of curiosity," Nancy said.

"During an art sting operation in New York," Carson Drew continued, "the police raided a well-known dealer. Behind some of the canvases in his back room, they found stolen canvases tacked underneath. Several came from the Cabbott."

Nancy whistled. "Was Dr. Morrison involved?"

135

"There was no proof against Morrison. And the Cabbott had already sold some of its paintings to this dealer to raise funds to buy new work."

"Was anyone charged?" Nancy asked.

"The New York dealer, yes," her father replied. "But he wouldn't reveal his accomplices. No one at the Cabbott was charged, but as I said, there was a lot of suspicion. The curious thing was that Dr. Morrison resigned shortly afterward. Then he went to Emerson."

Nancy's mind sifted through this information. The story was very familiar. Nancy remembered Debbie taking inventory the night of the robbery. A shipment of paintings was going out of the Emerson College Art Museum to a dealer sometime soon. If Dr. Morrison had been involved in the theft at the Cabbott, could he be using the same ploy here at Emerson? Did he plan to hide *First Kiss* in the next shipment of paintings? He might have used the same method of tacking the *First Kiss* behind another canvas.

"This information may be critical, Dad. You've been a great help."

"If Dr. Morrison is involved in art theft, the directors at the Cabbott will certainly regret hushing up the affair there. Be careful, Nancy. Art theft is serious business."

"I'll be careful, Dad," Nancy promised. She hung up and found George doing pushups in front of an exercise tape in the den. "I'm heading over to the art museum," Nancy told her. "I think Dr. Morrison made a trip out to Lincoln Valley this afternoon."

"So Bryan really is in the clear?" George smiled, then looked concerned. "I'd better go with you. Dr. Morrison could be dangerous."

Nancy glanced at the clock. It was five-forty. "The museum closes in twenty minutes—we'd better hurry."

Minutes later Nancy was driving up the hill. It had started to pour again as she pulled into a space on the far side of the lot behind a large camper. She grabbed her red umbrella from the trunk as she and George dashed for the museum entrance. They passed the black sports car with personalized plates.

"How do you know Dr. Morrison tried to kill us?" George asked, huddling under the umbrella.

"Well," Nancy said, pointing to Morrison's car, "remember that bale of hay in the road?" Morrison's tires were thick with mud, and embedded in the mud were strands of hay. "That's our first bit of proof. Everything else is circumstantial."

"I don't get it, Nancy," George said, shivering under the umbrella. "Why would he try to hurt us if he has the painting?"

"Beats me," Nancy said. "But I want to check out those paintings that are being shipped out. I need to get into the storage room. Here's my plan."

George bent her head closer to Nancy's, listening carefully.

Nancy waited on one side of the entry doors while George entered the museum. As soon as she was inside, George began to stagger, half collapsing against the front desk. A young girl— a student, Nancy guessed—was behind the desk. "I'm going to faint," George gasped. "Please, help me."

The girl ran around the desk and helped George to a wooden bench across the foyer. George moaned, "Can I lie down somewhere? Just for a moment?"

"The staff lunchroom has a couch," the girl offered helpfully. Leaning on the girl's shoulder, George limped around the corner.

Perfect. Nancy silently applauded. She hoped that George could keep the girl occupied for a few minutes. Nancy went directly to the receptionist's desk. She had seen Dr. Morrison put the storage room key back in the drawer Sunday afternoon. Pulling a small drawer on the right, Nancy saw several keys, each one labeled. Nancy sorted through them quickly. "Storeroom, storeroom," she muttered. There it was.

After grabbing the key, Nancy raced to the storage room. She pressed her ear against the door but heard nothing. She knocked. No answer. After unlocking the door, she tiptoed in, and locked the door behind her.

Paintings were stacked everywhere. How would she ever go through all of them? Then Nancy remembered that *First Kiss* was small. If it was there at all, it would be tacked behind one of the smaller paintings. She found two canvases, one a painting of a snow-covered house, the other of water lilies. With her pocketknife, Nancy pried the snow scene from its frame. Then she carefully removed several of the tacks holding the canvas to its wooden stretcher. There was only one canvas.

Disappointed, Nancy tackled the second painting, removing the picture from its frame. Her heart beat fast when she saw two canvases tacked to the wooden stretcher, the edge of one peeking out behind the first. Nancy could hear her heart pounding. She carefully removed the tacks on one side of the stretcher and peered at the canvas underneath. It was a landscape with cows in it.

So she was on the right track. She hadn't found *First Kiss,* but she felt she was very close.

All at once Nancy understood why Dr. Morrison had fired Debbie the night of the robbery. It had nothing to do with *First Kiss.* It was because Debbie had been working on an inventory of the paintings going out of the museum. Morrison must have been afraid Debbie would discover what he was doing.

Go slow, Nancy cautioned herself. You have to find *First Kiss* and soon. George can't pretend to be fainting forever. Nancy found another small canvas. Finally, behind a group of dusty statues, she came across it. Exactly the right size. Nancy wrestled the canvas from its frame, then began pulling tacks, removing the canvas from its

wooden stretcher. Then suddenly there it was—
First Kiss. Nancy whistled softly under her
breath. This was a painting she would never
forget.

A key turned in the lock, and the storage room
door opened. Nancy's heart leaped to her throat
as she searched frantically for a place to hide.
Holding *First Kiss* close, she scurried behind a
large draped statue, pulling the dusty curtain
over her head as well.

The footsteps—Nancy was sure there were
two people—approached the spot where *First
Kiss* had been hidden. Suddenly an angry cry
went up. "It's gone!" Nancy recognized the
voice. It was Dr. Morrison's. "Search this
room!" he commanded.

Nancy clutched *First Kiss* to her chest, trying
not to breathe. The dust tickled her nose, and she
felt a sneeze coming on. Scrunching up her face,
she willed the sneeze away.

Through the drape she saw a shadow creep
nearer and nearer. Nancy braced herself as the
drape was pulled off. She was face-to-face with
Dr. Morrison—a pistol leveled directly at her
heart.

Chapter
Fifteen

"WHY, NANCY DREW," Dr. Morrison said, keeping the pistol trained on her. Jenkins, the maintenance man, scowled over the curator's shoulder. "What a surprise, seeing you here." Dr. Morrison smiled.

"You're the thief," Nancy said. "You stole this from Rina's car. You sabotaged the bridge."

"Yes, Nancy. So I didn't expect to find you here. Now I have a problem. How to dispose of you and George and Rina, too." He looked around. "A pity George isn't here with you."

Fear shot through Nancy. She hoped George had made it out of the museum before closing time. "Why did you try to kill us?" she asked.

"You know too much." He spoke so calmly that it was hard for Nancy to believe he was plotting murder. "What does Rina know about you?" Nancy asked, stalling for time.

Dr. Morrison's eyes narrowed. "Didn't she tell you? Well, it doesn't matter. You've discovered too much by yourself. You see, some months ago, Rina discovered my—my side business, you might call it. After she copied a drawing in the Morgan exhibit for me, Rina happened to visit the Morgan Museum. Unfortunately, she saw her own drawing on the wall."

"You used Rina to create a forgery."

"Yes," the curator said, smiling. "Her copies were excellent. So I asked her to copy a particularly valuable drawing, and I substituted it for the original. But Rina was not happy when she discovered what I'd done. A pity—forgery could have become quite profitable for her."

"Why didn't she go to the police?"

"Rina was smart enough to realize that it would be her word against mine. Who would you believe?" The curator shrugged. "But you worried me, Nancy. I was afraid that your questions might get Rina to say too much. So when you left the museum today, I followed you. The rain made for nice camouflage."

"And you tried to kill us," Nancy said. "But why didn't you just come into the cabin?"

"I considered it, but then an older woman arrived. And, frankly, I prefer indirect methods —accidents that can't be traced."

"Who makes your copies now?"

"Someone almost as good as Rina, but not quite."

"If you believe Rina is so talented, why didn't she win the art contest?" If only someone would come. But who? Nancy's heart sank. Bryan wasn't working this evening. He was at dinner with Ian Sanders. Ned had no idea where Nancy was, and Nancy only hoped that George had made it safely out of the museum.

"Rina is very talented," Dr. Morrison admitted. He acted amused, as if he understood Nancy's delaying tactic perfectly. "But her contest entry was a childish mess." He glanced at his watch. "Enough talk. I have an important delivery to make. Jenkins," he said to the maintenance man, "we'll leave her in the basement for the time being."

Pressing the gun into Nancy's back, Jenkins walked Nancy out of the storage room down the corridor to the metal door at the end of the hall. They descended the cement steps into the basement. There, Jenkins put a gag in her mouth and tied a rope tightly around her wrists and ankles and put her behind the furnace. "You won't be going anywhere," Jenkins muttered, giving the rope a jerk.

Behind the furnace Nancy couldn't see Jenkins leave. But she heard his footsteps on the stairs. Then the light went out, and the steel door shut with a solid clang.

What now? As Nancy struggled with the ropes

binding her, her eyes grew accustomed to the dark. Suddenly a head of spiky blond hair popped out from behind some boxes piled across from the furnace. Even in the dim light of the basement Nancy would know that hair anywhere. Jamie! Without a word Jamie hurried to Nancy's side, quickly removing her gag. "My hands next," Nancy whispered. "What are you doing here?"

"When I ran from you and Debbie, I needed a place to hide," Jamie told her, untying the rope. "Dr. Morrison is the bad guy?"

Nancy filled Jamie in quickly as the girl unwound the last rope from Nancy's feet. "And I'm sure it's *First Kiss* he's about to deliver," Nancy concluded, rubbing her hands and feet until the circulation returned. "We'd better move fast. You'll help me?"

Jamie nodded vigorously.

At the top of the steps Nancy inched open the steel door. The museum was as still as a tomb. She motioned Jamie to follow her into the women's rest room. Nancy hopped up on the radiator. Through the window she watched Dr. Morrison place a package into the trunk of his car. It was the size of *First Kiss*. A second later the car roared off.

A door creaked behind them. Jamie gripped Nancy's hand as they watched the door of a closet swing open. Nancy laughed joyfully when she saw the occupant. Stepping out from the mops and buckets, George emerged, holding a red umbrella. "I heard your voices," George said. "After I recovered from my 'fainting spell,' I hid. I wasn't going to leave you alone in this creepy place."

Nancy grinned. "Thanks, George. You're the best." Glancing back out the window, Nancy saw the museum security guard outside. Where had the guard been when she needed him? No matter. The guard wouldn't be any help—he wasn't likely to believe the museum curator was a thief. "Follow me," she directed, jumping down from her perch.

Because Nancy suspected that Jenkins might still be lurking in the museum, the girls crept silently out to the main entry hall. Nancy tiptoed toward the museum's doors, with George and Jamie behind her.

"As soon as those doors open, the alarm will go off," she whispered. "George, go hide in the bushes until the police come—then tell them everything. Jamie, would you come with me?"

Nancy turned the latch and pushed. An ear-splitting alarm screamed. George raced for the bushes while Jamie ran with Nancy to her Mustang. "Wow—what happened to your car?" the younger girl asked.

"I'll explain later," Nancy said. "We've got to stop Dr. Morrison before it's too late." Nancy drove to the President Hotel, two blocks off Main Street. Leaving Jamie in the car, she ran inside to the front desk.

"Mr. Sanders has just checked out," the desk clerk informed her.

"I must find him," Nancy said firmly.

"Try the airport. He had a flight tonight."

"Thanks. Could you please call the police?" Nancy asked. "Ask for Sergeant Weinberg and tell him the *First Kiss* is at the airport."

"Is this a joke, miss?"

"It's no joke," Nancy said, deadly serious. "Please make the call." Nancy watched the woman pick up the phone, then raced back to the car.

Jamie leaned over and opened the door.

Nancy knew the airport's location from previous visits. But the traffic and slick streets made driving difficult. Would they make it in time? She glanced over at Jamie. The girl said nothing but had an expectant look on her face. Nancy hoped that her guess was right—that the airport was in fact where Dr. Morrison was headed.

When she pulled into the airport's parking lot, she told Jamie to look for a black sports car with MORRISON license plates.

"There it is!" Jamie shouted. Nancy nodded. Then she drove out to the edge of the field. A man was descending the metal stairway of a small, single-engine prop plane, the propeller already turning. It was Dr. Morrison. The delivery had taken place.

Opening her purse, Nancy pulled out her pocketknife. "Here—for slashing Dr. Morrison's tires," she told Jamie. Jamie stared at Nancy and then at the knife. Then she scrambled out of the Mustang and took off for the sports car.

Nancy headed for the airport's single runway. She reached it just as the plane began to taxi toward her. Nancy steered straight for it.

Part of Nancy knew she was acting crazy. But another part of her was infuriated with Dr. Morrison. He had the makings of a cold-blooded murderer, and Nancy was determined to stop him. The plane continued to taxi toward Nancy's Mustang, gathering speed. Nancy drove forward, sheets of rain dousing her windshield.

If the plane didn't stop, Nancy would have to veer off and let the police at the other end deal with Sanders. She decided to hold out until the last possible second. The plane bore down on her, but something inside Nancy refused to give up and turn the wheel. In another second it would be too late.

Suddenly the plane slowed, brakes squealing, water spraying out from its tires. It came to a jolting stop, nose to nose with the Mustang. Jumping out of his cockpit, the pilot shook his fists angrily.

Nancy smiled in relief when she saw the police cars zoom onto the field. The pilot bolted, but the squad car gave chase. One police car headed for her and stopped. Sergeant Weinberg leaped out. Nancy sprinted toward him and pointed out Dr. Morrison hurrying across the parking lot to his car. "That's the thief!" she told the sergeant, who started after him. "But don't worry," Nancy said, and explained about the tires. "Jamie's hiding over there in the bushes. Maybe we'd better rescue her before Morrison spots her."

"So it's a wrap-up," Dean Jarvis said the next day after hanging *First Kiss* in its place on the museum wall. "And we have you to thank." He beamed at Nancy.

"I had a lot of help, Dean Jarvis," Nancy said. Standing at Nancy's side, Ned gave her hand a squeeze. Also gathered round were George, Bryan, Michael Jared, and Debbie. Nancy couldn't help but notice how Michael was looking at Debbie. And for the first time she realized Debbie bore a slight resemblance to the girl in *First Kiss.*

"I'm afraid I was overly impressed by Morrison's credentials, since the Cabbott is such a major museum," Dean Jarvis confessed. "I should have checked his references more carefully. I've learned an important lesson."

Michael turned to Nancy. "I don't know how to thank you," he said, staring deeply into her eyes. For exactly one second Nancy imagined that she was the girl in *First Kiss,* Michael's inspiration. Then she tore herself away and looked at Ned. He was smiling at her, his eyes filled with love. Nancy turned back to Michael. He was a handsome, fascinating man who had needed her help, but he wasn't Ned.

"What will happen now?" George asked.

"I spoke with Sergeant Weinberg a short while

ago," Nancy answered. "Dr. Morrison, Jenkins, and Sanders face criminal charges. Rina will be prosecuted, too, but the authorities are likely to be lenient because she's agreed to testify against Dr. Morrison in the earlier forgery."

"What about Jamie?" Ned asked.

"Debbie took Jamie back to the halfway house last night," Dean Jarvis told them.

"Mrs. Shephard is making sure Jamie gets more intensive counseling, and I told Jamie if she worked on her high school equivalency degree, she can apply to Emerson next fall," Debbie informed them. Then she took Nancy aside a moment. "I spoke with Michael and he arranged to pay for those art supplies Jamie took."

As the group drifted out of the museum, Nancy watched, amazed: Bryan was inviting George to a climbing trip the next weekend; Dean Jarvis had asked Debbie to temporarily take over as curator of the museum; Michael was taking Debbie to lunch to celebrate. Romance and good fortune seemed to be in the air. Nancy turned to find Ned.

"Hi, gorgeous," he said, stepping up behind her.

She leaned back against his chest and let out a sigh. "One more case over and done with."

"Almost. There's one detail unexplained," Ned said as they walked into the sunshine hand in hand. "What about that EC ticket stub?"

"That bothered me, too," Nancy admitted.

"But here's my theory. When Rina stole Bryan's climbing gear, she took his windbreaker, too. He'd worn it to the EC concert."

"And he put the ticket stub in his pocket."

"Right. Rina wore the jacket when she skated across campus—remember the hooded figure? She must have had it on the roof. The stub fell out."

"Brilliant, Nancy." Ned gave Nancy a big hug. "Dean Jarvis has a lot to thank you for."

"Actually," Nancy said, a twinkle in her eye, "it's Michael who should be thanking me now."

"Him again?"

"Yup," Nancy pointed to the parking lot. Michael was climbing into Debbie's white Subaru. "I didn't just find his painting. I may have helped him find the girl of his dreams."

Ned threw back his head and laughed. "Like I said, Drew, positively brilliant."

Nancy's next case:

One of River Heights's richest and most respected citizens, Charles Pierce, has fallen in love . . . and fallen out with his family. He asked his beautiful and much younger house-keeper, Nila, to marry him, and his heirs fear getting cut out of his will. But Pierce now fears for Nila's life, and he asks Nancy to investigate the threat. With all of Pierce's money at stake, there's no shortage of suspects—including his very handsome son, Philip. And Nancy has to wonder whether Philip's interest in her stems from affection, greed, or both. Either way, he spells trouble, and Nancy knows one thing for sure: by taking on this case, she's inherited a houseful of danger . . . in *For Love or Money,* Case #112 in The Nancy Drew Files℠.

By Carolyn Keene

Nancy Drew is going to college.
For Nancy, it's a time of change....A change
of address....A change of heart.

**FOLLOW NANCY'S COLLEGE
ADVENTURES WITH THE NEW
NANCY DREW ON CAMPUS SERIES**

Nancy Drew on Campus™#1:
❏ New Lives, New Loves......52737-1/$3.99

Nancy Drew on Campus™#2:
❏ On Her Own.....................52741-x/$3.99

THE HARDY BOYS CASEFILES